For all the Christmas lovers out there - may this book bring you joy all year long!

1

"*Die Hard* is absolutely a Christmas movie," I said, popping a french fry into my mouth. "To suggest anything different is ridiculous."

"You can't be serious." Estelle Adler, geriatric extraordinaire and my best friend, finished chewing a bite of her BLT and took a sip of water. "How can you say that *Die Hard* is in the same league as *It's A Wonderful Life* or *A Christmas Carol*? There's so much blood!"

I shrugged, twirling a piece of dark, curly hair around my finger. "I don't make the rules. All I know is that if you don't have *Die Hard* as part of your Christmas movie rotation, you're doing something wrong."

Estelle waved her hand flippantly and shook her head. "Ridiculous. I think this is something we're going to have to agree to disagree about."

"Ooh, what are we disagreeing about now?" Eddy, a server at the Hemlock Inn's bistro, strode up to our table and took my empty plate, stacking Estelle's plate on top, an elf's hat perched jauntily on his head.

"Simone over here has the audacity to claim that *Die*

Hard is a Christmas movie," Estelle said, leaning back in her seat and crossing her arms, her eyes narrowed in her lined face.

"Well, she's right. *Die Hard* is obviously a Christmas movie." Eddy shifted our dirty plates in his hands so he could better balance them.

"Are you serious?" Penny, the other server at the bistro, called out from across the dining room. She set down the dishes she was delivering to another table and hurried over to Eddy's side. "No way is *Die Hard* a Christmas movie. There's so much blood!"

"That's what I said!" Estelle leaned forward in her seat with a big grin on her face, as if Penny's agreement automatically meant she was right. She brushed a strand of white hair out of her face.

I smiled, watching my friends and employees argue the merits of *Die Hard* as a Christmas movie. I hadn't realized I was starting such a contentious conversation when I first brought it up, but it was always fun to see what random topic would set everyone off and derail any serious work or clearing of dishes. As long as no one got too up in arms about the disagreement, I was happy to let the bickering continue.

It was just after the breakfast rush, so the bistro at the Hemlock Inn wasn't extremely busy. Estelle had stopped by for breakfast with me like she did often, though her husband Miles hadn't been able to join us this time. He'd hurt his hip a few days ago and was on bed rest.

"Nothing that'll kill him!" Estelle had joked when she'd shown up to the inn and explained what was going on, but I could see the look in her eyes. Her husband didn't often get hurt or sick, but she was worried about him and how long it was taking for him to heal.

Still, I was glad to see Estelle laughing now, less caught up in what was going on with Miles. I wondered if he would side with his wife on this argument, or if he had the correct assessment of the true merits of *Die Hard* and its obvious placement as one of the top Christmas movies.

It was my second holiday season as owner of the Hemlock Inn, and I was looking forward to more relaxing this year. Last year, my role as owner of the inn was still new, as I'd only just arrived in Pine Brook over the summer, and I hadn't quite felt at ease in my new position. I'd spent most of last December scrambling to keep up with all the guests, battling icy snow and freezing temps, and alleviating my stress after work with a bottle of wine.

This year, my confidence levels were high and I knew I could handle whatever the inn threw at me. Running the inn no longer terrified me, I was in a happy, secure relationship, and we hadn't had a dead body in months. All in all, it was turning out to be a very pleasant holiday season.

A glance at the clock on the wall, partially obscured by a drooping garland hanging from the ceiling above, had me taking a final sip of my hot cocoa and standing up. "I need to check on things at the front desk," I told Estelle, resting my hand on her shoulder to get her attention. "Tell Miles I hope he feels better."

"Thanks, dear," Estelle said, waving half-heartedly, then turning her attention back to arguing with Eddy and Penny about the merits of *The Nightmare Before Christmas* as a Christmas movie.

Fortunately, the front lobby was quiet and devoid of bickering staff members. Tracy Williams, the inn's general manager and one of my close friends, stood behind the front desk, flipping through the mail. She'd just finished setting out a few bowls of cinnamon-scented pine cones around the lobby, and I took in a deep breath as I walked over to her.

The older woman was a few inches taller than me, with skin several shades darker than my brown cheeks, and with long dreadlocks currently in a braid that hung heavy down her back. A silver nose ring poked out from her dark skin.

"Oh, thank goodness, there you are," she said, straightening up at my approach. "Do you mind keeping an eye on things up here? I need to use the bathroom."

"Of course," I said, hurrying over to her side. "I'm sorry, I was having breakfast with Estelle in the bistro—I would've come out sooner if I knew you needed a break." I reached down to give Lola the beagle a scratch on her head, grinning at the sight of a Christmas bow hooked around her collar.

Tracy waved her hand flippantly. "It's okay. I was going to come find you if you didn't come out soon. We should look at bringing on more of the seasonal staff soon, now that things are picking up for the holidays. I can't wait until Nadia is back from her cruise."

I nodded my agreement, waving as Tracy scurried away to the bathroom. Nadia, who normally helped out at the front desk and whatever else we needed her for, was on a two-month cruise with her boyfriend, Christos. The pair had been long-distance for years, always missing each other when they tried to meet up or take trips together. A couple months ago, he'd finally shown up to the inn, surprising her with a visit, and proving to me that he actually existed.

After that visit, Nadia had put her foot down about their long-distance status and had asked for more from their relationship. Christos' solution had been a two-month cruise across the world, which just happened to keep Nadia away from the inn during one of our busiest seasons.

Given how happy Nadia was when she'd told us the

news, I'd tried not to let my frustration show since we were now down a staff member during the holiday season. She'd been gone since the beginning of November and would hopefully return after New Year's—assuming Christos didn't propose and convince her to move to Greece with him.

All month, with the Christmas season in full swing, I'd been dreading the possibility of Nadia not returning to the inn, and her silence the last few weeks hadn't helped. She was good at her job, even if she spent a lot of time on her phone texting Christos, and it was hard to find a good replacement in a town as small as Pine Brook.

Still, Tracy was right that we should find more seasonal help to alleviate the pressure over the holidays, and I made a note to myself to call the staffing agency we used this week to see if anyone from one of the nearby towns was looking for work this time of year.

Tracy strolled back into the lobby after a few minutes, taking a bite from an apple she must've picked up in the bistro. She fiddled with an ornament on the ten-foot-tall tree we'd set up near the fireplace, straightening it out. She'd spent the entirety of the first weekend after Thanksgiving setting up the Christmas tree and other decorations in the lobby, and I'd discovered her love for this holiday.

This pine tree was gorgeous, towering over the guests and eliciting glee from the children staying at the inn. It mostly reminded me of how bereft of decorations my apartment currently was. With how busy things were at the inn, I hadn't even had a chance to set up a tree or put up lights, and the holiday would be here soon. Hopefully the stores would still have decorations in stock once I got around to making my apartment more festive.

"Thanks," Tracy said, joining me behind the front desk

and continuing to flip through the mail. "Listen, I wanted to talk about Isabella..."

I smirked as her voice trailed off. Isabella Rodriguez was an investor who'd offered us financial support earlier this year, allowing us to add a spa to the inn. Tracy and Isabella had been romantically involved for months, but Tracy still struggled to talk about her as a girlfriend. I'd always figured Tracy hadn't completely moved on from her relationship with my Aunt Sylvia. Nonetheless, Tracy and Isabella were adorable together, always laughing and holding hands, and I didn't want to do anything to discourage Tracy from leaning into that relationship.

"What about her?" I asked, turning my attention to our weekly ledger, skimming over the words but not really reading anything. I just didn't want Tracy to feel the pressure of my eyes on her while she tried to articulate what she had to say about Isabella.

"She and I have been discussing plans for next year," Tracy went on, her gaze still down on the mail. "You know how she's a big traveler, right? Since investing in the Hemlock and, well, getting involved with me... she hasn't done as much traveling as she used to. I keep telling her she should feel comfortable going on trips when she wants to, but she said she doesn't want to go anywhere without me."

A giant smile blossomed across my face at those words. Jeez, these two were too cute! I almost couldn't handle it.

"What are you thinking about for next year?" I asked, keeping my tone steady. Once Nadia was back from her cruise, I'd be more than happy to give Tracy a couple weeks off to travel with her glamorous girlfriend. Tracy had barely taken any time off since Sylvia died and I'd taken over the inn, as she wanted to make sure I had help in case anything new came up. But as my confidence in my ability to run the inn grew, so did my comfort with not needing as much help from the people around me.

"We haven't confirmed anything yet," Tracy said hurriedly. "I wanted to talk to you about it first, of course. But Isabella has this six-month itinerary she created years ago that she's always wanted to take advantage of, traveling around to a bunch of different countries, and she thinks I might enjoy going with her."

My eyebrows shot up at her words. *Six months*? That was way more than the two weeks I'd been expecting. Could the inn even survive without Tracy for six months? Could *I* survive without her for that long?

I didn't want to immediately shut down her idea, but I was starting to freak out at the possibility of her being gone for so long. I opened my mouth to respond—scrambling to think of something to say—when the bell over the front door tinkled as someone entered the lobby. Not wanting a guest to see us bickering over Tracy's ginormous vacation request, I plastered on a smile and turned my attention to the person approaching the front desk.

My stomach dropped to my knees as my mother came to a stop in front of me, a giant smile on her face. "Surprise!"

2

"Mom," I managed to stammer out. "W-what are you doing here?"

"Well, I'm here to see my daughter, of course. And to finally see this lovely inn of hers." My mom turned to Tracy and held out her hand. "Henrietta Evans. Pleasure to meet you."

Tracy snapped her jaw shut, practically picking it up off the floor, and shook my mom's hand. "Nice to meet you, too. I'm Tracy, the inn's general manager. I didn't realize Simone's mom was stopping by this week."

"Neither did she," my mom said with a wink. "I thought I'd surprise her before the holidays. Your father is in Holland this month for a conference, and Chrissy and Mark took Hannah to Hawaii for the Christmas holidays. The clinic is shut down until the new year, and I didn't want to spend Christmas all by myself, so I thought I'd come see the Hemlock!"

"But Christmas isn't for two weeks…Why are you here so early?"

My mom shrugged. "Like I said, your father is gone, and

honestly, I got bored alone at home. I would've said something sooner, but I thought it would be fun to surprise you."

"We're thrilled you're here," Tracy said, pushing her way back into the conversation. "Who doesn't love a little holiday surprise? And I see you brought enough bags for the trip, too."

It was true; my mom had lugged in two large suitcases and a duffle bag across her back. Eddy came out of the bistro at that moment, presumably looking for us, and Tracy waved him over.

"Eddy, this is Simone's mom, Henrietta Evans," Tracy said, introducing the two of them. "Do you mind helping get her things upstairs?" Tracy flipped through the leather ledger on the front desk that we used for tracking guests each week. "Looks like we've got space in room ten." Tracy reached under the front desk and pulled out the key to the room, passing it to Eddy. "Eddy here will help you get settled," Tracy added to my mom.

"What excellent service," Mom said with a smile. Eddy grabbed her bags, and the two of them headed up the stairs together, chatting. Eddy didn't look too pleased about being roped into a bellhop position, but the opportunity to grill my mom for details about me was too good for him to pass up.

Once they'd left the lobby, Tracy turned to me. "Another family member showing up randomly, without any notice? What is going on with the women in your family?"

I shrugged. I was as lost as Tracy was. My sister, Chrissy, had done something similar last year, showing up randomly and without a good explanation. Turned out, she'd been having trouble in her marriage and needed to get away for a while. Unfortunately, we'd gotten caught up in a murder investigation involving someone from her past, and I'd seriously started to wonder if my sister was a killer. But we'd managed to find the true culprit, and Chrissy left Pine Brook more determined to work on her marriage with her husband Mark.

According to my mom, though, my dad was simply out of town and she was lonely now that her clinic was closed. It hadn't seemed like she was lying about her real reasons for being here, so I had to believe that she was telling the truth. Still, why hadn't she called beforehand? Did she think I wouldn't want her to stay if she gave me a chance to say no?

"Do you think there's something wrong with your parents' marriage?" Tracy asked, reading my mind. "I mean, I know when Chrissy came, it was clear that she was having issues with Mark. Do you think the same thing is happening here?"

I shook my head. "No, it sounded like she was being truthful. And my dad does travel a lot for conferences. He's not normally gone over the holiday season, but he's always looking for a new way to expand his practice and make more connections. It wouldn't surprise me if he saw this as an opportunity to do just that."

"Why wouldn't your mom go with him? Holland seems like a lovely place to visit."

"She doesn't like the cold. Seems odd that she'd choose to leave California to come up to Washington during the winter holidays, but maybe she was truly lonely."

"She's a doctor, right? I'm surprised she was able to leave her hospital."

"She works at a small clinic, and they often shut down over the holidays. She probably asked for more time off, too."

"It's lucky we even had a room available at this point,"

Tracy said, flipping through the weekly ledger. "We're normally completed booked out this time of year."

"The Millers just checked out of room ten, remember? They're heading out on the holiday cruise up to Alaska and only stayed for a week, and no one else was booked in that room until January. I guess she's just got great timing." Had my mom shown up a day later, that room likely would've been snatched up by someone else.

"Does she...does she know about Sylvia and me?" Tracy asked, her voice soft.

My eyes widened. I'd completely forgotten about that. Not many people in town knew about Tracy's relationship with Sylvia, and Tracy didn't talk about it much since Sylvia had passed away. My mom and Aunt Sylvia had been estranged for a while, as well, so maybe Sylvia never told her.

I had memories of coming to the Hemlock with Chrissy when we were kids, running around the halls of the inn and undoubtedly bothering the guests. But at some point, we'd stopped visiting and our communication with Aunt Sylvia had petered off. We still occasionally exchanged birthday and Christmas cards with her, but I hadn't spoken to her in years when I got the call that she'd passed away and had left me the inn. I'd assumed that my mom hadn't spoken to her in that time, either, which likely meant she wasn't aware of the relationship that Sylvia had started after my Uncle Tim passed away.

"I doubt it," I said. "The two of them hadn't been very close in recent years. Did Sylvia ever talk about my mom?"

"Sometimes, though not often. She talked about you and Chrissy quite a bit, but I got the sense that you all were mostly estranged. She never said anything about a huge fight or anything like that. Family can be complicated, though, so I never pushed her to talk about it when it seemed like she didn't want to."

A letter from Sylvia flashed through my mind. It was currently locked in a drawer in my office, and I hadn't looked at it in at least six months. In it, Sylvia had explained her reasoning behind leaving me the inn and what she hoped I did with it. When I'd found it after being at the inn for a few days, I'd been really struggling with whether I could run this place without Sylvia. Reading the letter, and seeing all the confidence she'd had in me, it had helped me to feel more confident about becoming the owner of the Hemlock Inn.

In the letter, she'd also referenced the estrangement with my mother, but she hadn't given many details. Instead, she'd told me to talk to Henrietta myself to get those details. I hadn't ever brought it up with my mom, as it had never seemed like the right time. However, now she was here in my inn, in what used to be Sylvia's inn. I didn't even think she'd been here since Chrissy and I were kids, twenty years ago.

But now that she'd shown up and was going to be here for several weeks, maybe this was my opportunity to talk to her about the contents of the letter and learn about what had caused the two women to be estranged for so long.

"I'm sure everything will be fine," Tracy said. "Maybe this is good. It's finally your opportunity to talk to your mom about all those things you haven't had a chance to talk to her about. Besides, she's going to be here for a while; do you really want to spend the next two and a half weeks walking on eggshells around her?"

Tracy was right, as much as I didn't want to admit it. Just because my mom and I had butted heads in the past, didn't mean that this visit needed to be anything like that. I was an adult with a successful business, and I didn't need to let any of my childhood insecurities get to me.

"I sure hope you're right," I said as my mom made her way down the stairs back to the lobby. "Otherwise, these next few weeks are going to be very awkward indeed." Hopefully her visit wouldn't make things weird with Christmas, either.

"I'm going to go check on the spa," Tracy murmured as my mom approached the front desk, not wanting her to overhear. "Still not sure how I want to act around her, so my solution is to avoid her." She dashed away from the front desk before I had a chance to stop her. At some point, those two were going to have to talk about Tracy's relationship with Sylvia, but I wasn't going to force her to do it now.

"Well, my room is very lovely," my mom said as she came to a stop at the front desk. She'd pulled her dark curls up into a high bun, and her freshly-washed dark cheeks were a mirror-image of mine. Chrissy, my mom, and I had looked like twins ever since we were kids. "It's been years since I've been back here, but I do love all the changes you've made," she went on. "Sylvia would've been proud to see all the hard work you've put into this place."

"Thank you, that's kind of you to say. We actually expanded with a spa earlier this year, as well," I added. "Would you like to see it?"

"I would love to!"

I led my mom through the inn, pointing out some of the other features we'd added in the time since I'd taken over the inn. I brought her back to the spa (making sure to avoid bumping into Tracy, who stayed out of sight), and showing off the different treatment rooms, nice-smelling products, and calming ambiance we'd managed to foster back here.

We ran into Estelle as we came back into the lobby. She quickly realized who I was with and introduced herself.

"Henrietta, isn't that right?" she asked, reaching out to shake my mom's hand. "I've heard so much about you. My name is Estelle Adler."

"Great to meet you," Mom said, returning the handshake, her smile wide. "Wow, I guess it's true about that small-town welcome—everyone knows who you are!"

I laughed. "Well, everyone knows who you are when you're at your daughter's inn. But yes, lots of people know each other in Pine Brook."

"Very different from Los Angeles, I'm sure," Estelle said. "I've always wanted to visit, but I've never had the chance."

"After such a nice welcome for me here, you must come visit as soon as you can," Mom replied. "I'll show you around all the sights!"

"Are you leaving to check on Miles?" I asked Estelle.

She nodded. "My husband," she explained to my mom. "He hurt his hip a few days ago, so the doctor has him on bed rest for a little while. He should be right as rain soon! I'm also going to bring some cookies to Kathleen," she added to me, holding up a bag filled with delicious treats from Hank, our chef. "She's been feeling a little sick, as well, so I thought I'd bring her something to cheer her up."

Kathleen was an eighty-year-old woman in town with more spunk than most people my age, and a close friend of Estelle's. She'd been welcoming to me when I'd first gotten to Pine Brook, and she always made it a point to stop and chat with me whenever we passed each other in town.

"Oh, I'm sorry to hear she's not feeling well, either," I

said, my brow furrowed with concern. "I hope there's not something going around."

Estelle flapped her hand nonchalantly. "No big deal. Just something that happens when you get old!" Her tone was light, though there was tension in her eyes as she spoke.

"Well, I don't want to keep you two from your tour," she went on, gesturing to my mom and me. "It was a pleasure to finally meet you, Henrietta, and I hope we get a chance to spend more time together while you're here."

"I would love that," my mom replied with a warm smile.

Estelle waved her goodbyes as she dashed out the front door. I couldn't help a chill of concern race down my spine as she left. Estelle spent so much time taking care of those around her, I just hoped she also took some time to slow down herself and not run herself ragged. She wasn't a spring chicken anymore, as much as she didn't want to admit it.

"What a kind woman," Mom said, interrupting my thoughts. "I'm really impressed with all of this. I'd love to see the bistro, as well. I'm feeling a bit peckish."

"Of course, let's get you something to eat." I guided her back to the bistro and settled her down at one of the tables, pushing concerns about Estelle to the back of my mind. She'd be upset if she knew I was letting worries about her get in the way of my mom's visit.

Penny hurried over to our table, setting down two glasses of water, her smile wide. "Hi there!" she said, sticking out her hand. "So great to finally meet Simone's mom!"

"Lovely meeting you, as well," she said, shaking hands with Penny. "I'm also very interested in this squash soup on the menu. I know it's technically still breakfast time, but I can't resist a seasonal soup."

"Of course," Penny said, scribbling down her order. "A

lot of our guests feel the same way about Hank's soups, actually. Simone, anything for you?"

"Just some coffee." And a reassurance that I could get through this visit without anything going wrong.

"You're not hungry?" my mom asked once Penny had left us alone, taking a sip of her water.

"I already ate. Now, tell me all about your flight. I hope everything went smoothly."

"Yes, no issues at all! I never realized how close Washington actually is to California. Such a quick trip."

"Hey, Simone, I hope I'm not interrupting anything." Nick Yoshida, my boyfriend and super attractive produce farmer, approached our table with a smile.

"Of course not," I said, relieved for the interruption. "This is Henrietta, my mom. Mom, this is Nick." I couldn't keep a smile from spreading across my face as I introduced them. My worlds were colliding, but it was starting to feel good.

"Pleasure to meet you," Mom said, shaking Nick's hand. "Simone's told me so much about you."

"She's said some wonderful things about you, too. I just came by to drop off an order in the kitchen, so I can't stay long. How long are you in town?"

"All the way through Christmas! We must make plans to get together soon."

"Yeah, that'd be pretty great," Nick said, his eyes warm. "I'm sure my father would love to meet you, as well. Why don't we plan to grab dinner sometime this week?"

"That would be lovely," Mom said.

"Simone, why don't you give me a call tonight, and we can plan something?"

I nodded my agreement, then Nick leaned down and gave me a quick kiss on the lips and left.

"Well, he seems like a lovely man," Mom said once we were alone. "I'm looking forward to getting to know him better while I'm here."

"He's pretty great." In fact, Nick was better than great—he was practically perfect. We'd been through some tough situations in our relationship, including, most recently, an unexpected visit from my ex-boyfriend. But he'd stayed committed to me during the entire time, and our relationship was even stronger now.

My mom leaned forward and lowered her voice. "When do you think he'll pop the question?"

I laughed. "Don't be so loud about it! Someone might overhear."

She leaned back and raised her hands in a placating gesture. "Not that I'm trying to put any pressure onto you or anything. You just seem really happy, and you seem to like your life up here. I just wonder what the next step might be for you."

Fortunately, Penny showed up at that moment with our food, offering me a reprieve from having to respond to my mom's question. She dug into her butternut squash soup while I took a sip of my coffee.

I wasn't upset with her for asking the question, but I did think it was a little early in our relationship to be considering marriage. We'd been dating for almost a year, and we'd gone through a lot of complicated situations together, but it still felt maybe a bit too soon for a wedding.

I was interested in having a conversation with him about potentially moving in together, though. He'd mentioned to me recently that his apartment lease was renewing soon, but he hadn't said anything one way or the other about what he was going to do with it. Currently, I lived on the floor below him, but even that sometimes felt too far apart. Should I ask him if he wanted to move in together? Was that moving too fast?

I was still a bit shaken up by my mom's surprise visit, but now that she was here, I may as well try to get into the Christmas spirit, and guide the conversation away from discussing the future of my relationship.

"I still need to find a gift for Nick. Maybe while you're here, we can go shopping for him together?" She'd probably bring up the future of our relationship again during that shopping trip, but maybe I'd be able to distract her with shiny objects and nice-smelling candles. She always loved an expensive candle.

My mom grinned broadly. "That sounds lovely. I'd like to get settled into my room today, and I'm sure you're busy with work, but we can definitely plan a mother-daughter shopping trip while I'm here!"

We hadn't had a mother-daughter shopping trip since I was a kid, but I appreciated her enthusiasm. Maybe this was what I needed to get excited about the holiday season.

While I wasn't ready to talk about the future of my relationship with Nick with my mom, there was another topic that I was eager to bring up with her: Sylvia's letter, and the history of their estrangement. When I'd first told her that Sylvia had passed away, she'd been sad but cryptic about their relationship. We'd all assumed that Sylvia had left me the inn, instead of Chrissy or my mom, because I'd always been more adrift and with less focus in my life.

That reason had been confirmed in the letter Sylvia had left me. But I still hadn't brought up the distance between the two of them because I'd wanted to give my mom space to grieve Sylvia's death and not push her to answer all my questions. Now that she was here, it felt like the perfect opportunity to bring it up again.

"You said you hadn't been back to the inn in years," I said as my mom finished off her soup. "Was the last time you were here when we took that family trip when I was in middle school?"

She shook her head, wiping her lips with her napkin. "That was the last time we came as a family, over the summer, but your father and I took a few weekend trips together when you were in high school, too. Sylvia would be very proud of how well you've managed to run this place, especially with the addition of the spa in the back. I know she always had high hopes for this place."

I leaned forward in my seat, gripping my hands around my coffee mug. "Why did you stop visiting? Did something happen with Sylvia?"

At those words, my mom's body visibly tensed, and she leaned away from me, dropping her gaze down to her bowl. She began fiddling with her spoon, scraping up the last bits of soup and popping it into her mouth. She didn't say anything for a moment.

"Nothing in particular," she finally said. "Your father and I got busy with work, and you girls were getting older and didn't want to make these visits anymore. It became less convenient to visit the inn."

I'd known that we'd spent less time with Sylvia as I'd gotten older, especially once I'd gone off to college. I hadn't given it much thought at the time because I'd been busy at school, but there had always been a cloud of tension over the family when Sylvia was brought up. Once I'd read Sylvia's letter, she'd confirmed that there was more going on between the two women, and now it seemed like my mom was trying to avoid the reason completely.

"You're sure there wasn't some big fight, or something? Some reason why you fell out of touch with her?" I asked.

She opened her mouth to respond, but the ringing of my phone interrupted her. "You better get that, dear," she said, leaning back in her seat.

I wanted to ignore whoever was on the other line and get my mom to talk to me about what had happened between her and Sylvia, but it was clear she wasn't interested in talking about it right now. Better to deal with this phone call and try again later.

Estelle's face flashed across my phone's screen. My face softened into a smile as I answered the call. "Hey there, how are you?"

"I need help." Estelle's voice was tight and high-pitched, like she was trying to keep herself from crying.

Any relaxation in my body immediately disappeared as I tensed up at Estelle's words and tone. "What's wrong? Where are you?"

"I'm at Kathleen's house. She... she's been hurt. The police... they say she's dead!"

3

"Stay where you are. I'll be right there." I hung up the phone, my thoughts spinning. "Mom, I'm sorry, but I have to go. One of my friends... Estelle says she's dead. I need to check on Estelle."

"Oh, dear! Well, I'll come with you to help make sure everything is okay."

"No, you don't need to do that. You should stay here and relax."

"I'm not going to be able to relax knowing that someone is dead! Listen to your mother, and let's go!"

With a sigh, I stood from the table and led her out of the bistro, waving to Penny that we were finished. I hated bringing my mom into such a somber situation, but I was secretly happy for the company. I didn't know what I was about to walk into when I got to Kathleen's home, but I was glad I wasn't doing it alone.

We were silent as we drove across town. I'd never been to Kathleen's home before, but I knew generally where she lived in town, and the firetruck and ambulance out front pointed directly to the right house. Estelle was standing on the porch, her arms wrapped around her small frame, gazing into the house through the open door. I parked my car across the street, out of the way of the emergency personnel, and my mom and I hurried over to Estelle. A wreath hung on the open front door.

"What happened?" I asked, pulling Estelle into me for a hug, wrapping my arms around the smaller woman. Her body shook as I held her close.

"I-I came over to bring her cookies." Estelle held up the bag, her hands shaking, and my mom gently took it from her. "When I got here... the police had just arrived... They said she's dead!"

Poking my head through the front door, I saw a cozy entryway with garland strung across a side table, frosted pine cones and twinkling lights nestled within the pine needles. The entryway led off to a living room, where most of the emergency personnel were gathered. A tall blonde woman stood a bit apart from them all, watching the scene and chewing on her thumbnail. She must've sensed my gaze, as she glanced up and looked my way, tears streaking down her cheeks.

I couldn't get a good look from where I was standing, but the people gathered in the living room still must've been dealing with Kathleen. What exactly had happened here?

Another cop walked past us, preparing to enter the house, and I reached out to stop her before she could go inside. "Excuse me, what's going on here? We came by to check on our friend."

The cop gave us each a look, her face unreadable. "Your friend is Kathleen Richards?" When I nodded, her face softened. "I'm sorry to have to tell you this, but your friend has passed away. She slipped down the stairs and hit her head."

Estelle cried out at those words, and my mom pulled her

close, softly patting the other woman's back as Estelle cried into her shoulder.

The cop gently led us away from the front door and down the porch steps, through Kathleen's front garden. Plastic candy canes, each two feet tall, lined the walkway. "I think it's best if you all head home. We still need to notify next of kin, so please keep this to yourselves. Can I get your names before you go, in case we have any follow up questions for you?"

"Yes, of course," I said, quickly identifying the three of us and our relation to Kathleen. The cop took down our names, then turned and went inside the house.

I led Estelle and my mom out onto the street and in the direction of my car. A few neighbors had come out of their homes and were watching the spectacle out front. I didn't want anyone bothering Estelle while she was dealing with her emotions, so I kept us a good distance away from the crowd. My mom had found a clean tissue in one of her pockets and passed it to Estelle, who wiped at her tears and took a few deep breaths.

"I'm so sorry about this," I said, pulling my friend into another hug. "Kathleen was a good woman."

"I can't believe she's gone," Estelle said, staring down at the tissue clenched in her hand. "We just talked yesterday."

"It's always so hard to lose a friend," my mom said, wrapping her arm around Estelle's shoulder and holding her steady.

"Who was that blonde woman inside?" I asked. "Her daughter?"

Estelle shook her head. "Kathleen's daughter is a brunette. I think that was her nurse, Paula something. She must've found Kathleen..." Her voice trailed off as more tears poured down her cheeks.

"It's going to be okay," I said, pulling Estelle in for another hug. My mom and I gently held her from both sides, patting her back in what I hoped was a soothing gesture.

After a few moments, Estelle straightened up. "I think I'll be okay. I just need a little time to process this. I better get home to Miles and make sure he's okay, too."

"Yes, of course, you should be with your husband right now. Do you want me to give you a lift home? I don't want you to have to drive right now." As I said the words, my phone buzzed from an incoming text message. Glancing at the screen, I groaned. "Shoot, I need to get back to the inn. I left Lola behind when I got your call, and apparently she ate some chocolate that a guest dropped. I might have to take her to the vet." I hated to leave Estelle alone like this, especially since she didn't seem to be in any condition to drive herself home, but I was also worried about my pup.

"I can bring her home," my mom said, wrapping her arm around Estelle again. "I'll give you a lift back and can make sure that your husband is doing okay, as well."

"Mom, are you sure? How will you get yourself back to the inn?"

"Don't worry about that. I can get a taxi or something. You should go, make sure Lola is okay. We'll be fine. Now, tell me, where is your car parked?" she said to Estelle, already turning the other woman away from me.

I took one last look at Kathleen's house before getting into my car, grateful that my mom and Estelle were taken care of.

A truck from the morgue had shown up, and Kathleen's body was being wheeled out on a stretcher, covered up by a black bag. Tears pooled in my eyes at the sight. Kathleen was a great woman, and she didn't deserve to die, especially not so suddenly like this from a fall. Estelle had known her for years, and the two women had been good friends. I hoped that she would take the time she needed to grieve the loss of her friend.

I found Penny sitting with Lola in the lobby, stroking her fur. "Is she okay?" I asked, hurrying over to the two of them, looking for signs of vomiting. Dogs and chocolate didn't mix well, and I'd probably have to take her to the vet.

Penny stood. "I'm sorry for the fire alarm text. She had a candy bar in her mouth, but it turns out it was only the wrapper, and we don't think she actually ingested any of the chocolate. I've been keeping an eye on her, but I think she's fine."

I let out a deep exhale, relieved that my dog was okay. I came over to the two of them and patted Lola's back. "Thanks for keeping an eye on her. I've got her now."

Penny nodded and ruffled Lola's fur, then headed back to the bistro. I sent a text to my mom, asking how Estelle was doing. Once I was certain that Lola was okay, I wanted to head back out to be with Estelle. She was in a lot of pain with Kathleen's death, and I wanted to be there for her.

Tracy approached the front desk with a few files in her hands. "There you are. Sorry about the urgent text. Penny didn't know if Lola was going to get sick, and she didn't realize I was back in the spa taking inventory, or else she would've had me help. But it looks like everything is okay here. Sorry for making you come back so quickly."

"That's fine," I said, giving Lola one last pat and standing up. "Glad to hear she didn't eat any chocolate."

"Did your mom go up to her room?" Tracy asked, flicking through a few of the files until she found what she was looking for.

"No, she's, um, with Estelle," I said. That cop had asked

us not to say anything about what we had seen today until they'd had a chance to talk to Kathleen's next of kin, so I didn't want to mention how upset Estelle was right now. "They're checking on Miles."

"Glad to see they seem to be hitting it off, your mom and Estelle. Did your mom say anything else about why she's in town?"

I shook my head. "It doesn't seem like there's anything wrong, but it's still surprising. Maybe I should text my dad and see if he knows what's going on."

"That's a good idea. I've got a handle on things up here if you want to go back to the office."

"Thanks, Tracy." I gave Lola one last pat on the head, then went off to my office in the back, sending off a text to my dad as I walked, checking in and making sure he at least knew that Mom was with me and not at home. His reply was quick.

She mentioned she was going to come visit you. Glad you both won't be alone for the holidays. Call me when you get a chance!

Well, at least that confirmed that there didn't appear to be anything wrong between the two of them. Maybe she was just here because she wanted to spend time with her daughter and not spend the holidays alone. Was that really so hard for me to believe?

There was one other person out there who might be able to give me a hint as to why my mother was in town. There wasn't a big time difference between Pine Brook and Hawaii, so I knew she'd be awake. I wasn't really sure why I was so suspicious of my mom's visit. It wasn't crazy to think that she might want to spend Christmas with her daughter, especially since the rest of our family was on other trips.

Still, her visit had me anxious—maybe because I wasn't

actually all that confident about my ability to run this inn, and I worried she might secretly be judging me?—and I wanted to make sure there wasn't some other reason why she was here, besides just wanting to spend Christmas with me. Yes, I was being paranoid, but I couldn't quite help it.

"Well, this is a surprise," Chrissy said when she answered my call. "I'm laying out on the beach right now. Normally, I wouldn't even pick up since I'm supposed to be relaxing, but Hannah wanted me to take a picture of her snorkeling."

I smiled at the image of my young niece in her snorkel gear, frolicking with sea turtles. "How's the weather? Bet it's nicer than the gray we've got here in Pine Brook."

"We actually had some rain in L.A. right before we left, so I was not too sad to leave that behind. So far, it's been sun, sun, and more sun. Not that I don't love talking to you, but I need to flip onto my back in about five minutes if I'm going to get an even tan. What can I do for you?"

I smiled and rolled my eyes. My sister was a distinguished college professor with more brains than most of the people likely staying at her resort, yet she never missed an opportunity to glamor herself up. Given our darker complexion, I didn't think a tan was super necessary for her, but I wasn't going to rain on her parade.

"Mom's in Pine Brook. She's staying at the Hemlock. Did you know about this?"

"What? No, of course not, or else I would've said something to you. When did she arrive?"

"This morning. Apparently, Dad is in Holland at some conference, and with you and Mark in Hawaii, she didn't want to spend the holidays alone, so she decided to come crash at my inn."

"Maybe she just wanted to spend the holidays with her

daughter. It has been a while since the two of you have spent time alone together, right? Besides, she hasn't seen the Hemlock since Sylvia gave it to you. Maybe she wants to take a walk down memory lane."

"Maybe..." Chrissy was making a lot of good points, and likely my own insecurities about running the inn were getting in the way. With Nadia gone, Tracy and I had been doing fine enough, but now that Tracy was considering a six-month vacation away from the inn, I was getting worried about my ability to keep things running smoothly. With my mom in town, I felt like a ten-year-old with her staring over my shoulder, checking my work.

I let out a sigh. "I'm probably reading too much into this. It's nice to see her, and it'll make Christmas feel more special, spending it with family. Something weird did happen, though. You know how there was always tension whenever Sylvia's name came up once we were in high school and college, right?"

"Of course. Mom always got so awkward when we talked about her."

"Well, I tried to bring that up with her earlier, and she shut down completely. It's like she doesn't want to talk about what really happened between them."

"Maybe she feels bad about it. Her sister is gone now, and she can't repair their relationship. She might regret letting all that time pass without resolving things with her."

That was a good point. Still, I couldn't get Sylvia's letter out of my head. She'd wanted me to talk to my mom about what had happened between the two of them, and I didn't want Henrietta to leave without figuring out what had really gone on.

"Any new murder cases these days?" Chrissy asked, pulling my attention back to our phone call.

"Jeez, Chrissy, you're supposed to be on vacation, not thinking about murder." My sister was obsessed with true crime documentaries and had had a crash-course in murder investigations when she'd visited Pine Brook last year and been accused of murder. I'd assumed that experience would've turned her off of the genre of true crime stories, but apparently she wasn't deterred.

"It's just a question! While I love Hawaii, things have been a little boring here. I brought a few mystery paperbacks with me and have been tearing through them all week."

"It is interesting that you ask about that, though," I said. "We did find a dead body today, though it doesn't look like murder." Since Chrissy was in Hawaii, I didn't think it would be a big deal to tell her what happened before next of kin had been notified. "Kathleen—she's an older woman who lived in town, I don't think you ever met her—she was found dead in her home earlier today. But it looks like she fell. She was older and getting unsteady. A very sad situation, but it seems like an accident. I mean, not all deaths equal murder, right?"

"Not in Pine Brook," Chrissy replied. "I wouldn't be too surprised to learn that there was more going on with this death."

Goodness, I sure hoped not. Kathleen's death was an accident, and I wasn't interested in considering any other possibilities right now.

4

I went back to the front desk, reading a text that had come in from my mom while I was talking with Chrissy. Estelle was taking a nap, and my mom was talking with Miles about his hip, to see if there was anything she could do to help with his recovery. I slipped my phone back into my pocket after replying with thanks for the update. It was good to hear that Estelle was resting—she'd had a chaotic day, and the impact of Kathleen's death was undoubtedly a lot to bear right now. I still wanted to check in on her myself and see how she was doing, but there wasn't much I could do if she were asleep. I'd check back in in an hour or so and see how she was doing.

My heart ached at the thought of Kathleen's death, but I didn't want to let my emotions overcome me while at work. I hadn't been close enough to Kathleen to feel like I needed to take any time off because of her death, but I'd make sure to take things easy while I was working, as I did feel the impact of her sudden loss of life.

Nick stood at the front desk when I returned to the lobby, and the tension eased out of my shoulders at the sight of him. I wasn't supposed to talk to people about Kathleen's death, but I couldn't keep all of this inside for very long. Nick wouldn't tell anyone if I shared it with him, and he might help make me feel better.

"Hey, I didn't think I'd see you again so soon," I said to Nick as I approached the front desk.

He jumped back from where he'd been talking to Tracy, his cheeks turning pink as he turned to me. He gripped a bundle of Christmas lights in his hands. "Hi, Simone, I didn't realize you were here. I, uh, I have to go. I'll call you later!" He quickly kissed my cheek, then dashed out of the inn before I had a chance to say anything.

"Uh, what was that all about?" I asked, turning back to Tracy.

She had a smirk on her face, which she quickly dropped, but she couldn't hide it fast enough. "Nothing. He was just, um, going over his delivery schedule for the week with me."

I narrowed my eyes at her, sensing that I was missing something. "But he normally does that with Hank since he's in charge of the bistro and making sure we have enough produce. Why would Nick talk to you about it?"

Tracy waved a hand in the air casually, as if brushing away my concerns like a bothersome fly. "Hank was busy setting out one of those rain mats from the back , so Nick thought he'd talk to me, instead. After the snow last night, everyone keeps trampling in water all over the floor, so I asked Hank and Eddy to put the mat down in front of the door up here."

There had been a light dusting of snow the night before, but the temperatures had warmed up enough this morning that the snow had started melting once people were waking up. For us, that meant dealing with soggy shoes as people came in and out of the inn.

"Hopefully we don't get too much more snow this early in the season. Remember last year, when that big storm rolled in right before Christmas, and we were all stuck inside for almost a week?"

Tracy laughed and rolled her eyes. "It wasn't that bad, though I'm not surprised the California kid can't handle the snow. A few years back, we had a major snowstorm and couldn't leave our houses for two weeks! Fortunately, we'd stocked up on enough food at the inn to keep everyone going through the snow storm, but Sylvia and I had to stay in her suite here because it was too hard to get home each night." Her eyes glazed over as she took a trip down memory lane in her head.

I cocked my head to the side, my thoughts drawn back to the sudden disappearance of my boyfriend. "Why did Nick have Christmas lights?"

Tracy shifted her weight between her feet and studied her nails. "He asked to borrow some so he could decorate the barn. Said he wanted to make the place cheerful for his workers, or something."

I narrowed my eyes. "Why wouldn't he ask me to borrow them?"

"Well," Tracy said slowly, not meeting my gaze. "You weren't here, but I was. So he, um, asked me instead. Listen, did your mom say anything about me or Sylvia while you were out?" Tracy asked, gnawing on one of her fingernails, something she only did when she was nervous.

I wasn't quite ready to move on from understanding why my boyfriend was borrowing the inn's Christmas lights, or why Tracy and Nick were acting so weird about it, but it didn't seem worth pushing the issue at this point. "No, she didn't say anything. You should just talk to her about your relationship. I'm sure she'd love to hear about your time with Sylvia."

"I dunno," Tracy said, looking down at the keyboard in front of her. "I don't want to make things weird for her. I mean, did she even know about our relationship? Or did she think that Sylvia was always single after your uncle passed away?"

I shrugged. "I'm not sure. Honestly, my mom isn't saying very much about Sylvia right now. But I don't think she'd be upset if you opened up to her about it."

"Maybe you're right. I'll think about it."

"Personally, I'm also feeling a little nervous about her visit. I texted my dad about it, and he was just happy to hear that she made it to Pine Brook. I called Chrissy, too, and she didn't know about this surprise trip, either. Do you think she's here to, I dunno, make sure I'm running this place correctly?"

"I think she's here to spend the holidays with her daughter, like she said. I'm sure she doesn't have some ulterior motive for being here."

"Maybe... I just want to impress her, you know? I want her to be proud of me and this inn."

Tracy reached out and gave my hand a squeeze. "I'm sure she is proud. You've done an amazing job here! You have nothing to worry about."

"I'm sure you're right." Still, it was hard not to keep my thoughts from racing about why my mom was really here.

She'd always held Chrissy and me to high standards and, while Chrissy had often met those standards, becoming a college professor, marrying a good man, having an adorable daughter, I always felt like I was falling short—dating a jerk who cheated on me, losing every job I tried, almost getting kicked out of my apartment in Los Angeles. I knew I'd done a good job with the inn and that Sylvia would be proud of me, but I still wasn't sure if I was living up to my mom's standards.

"It does feel like things are more hectic here than normal," I went on. "What with you not able to take a bathroom break earlier, and then me having to rush back to check on Lola. I'm happy that Nadia is able to have this time off to spend with Christos, but it's been tough not having her here, too. I never quite realized how much I relied on her to keep the ship sailing."

Tracy tilted her head to the side, her brow furrowed. "Really? I think things have been fine. I mean, sure, maybe it's a bit more hectic than normal, but it's always a crazy time over the holidays. I'm surprised to hear that you think it's been tough without Nadia around. From where I'm standing, you've been doing a really great job of managing everything."

My cheeks warmed at the compliment. "Thank you." Was she right, and all my anxieties were just in my head? Was I reading too much into my mom's visit and assuming she was holding me to a high standard that I'd actually set for myself?

"Have you had a chance to think about the trip I mentioned with Isabella?" Tracy asked, interrupting my spiraling thoughts. "I know it's a lot of time off, but I haven't had much time away from the inn the last few years, and Isabella is so excited to show me around to different places."

Oh man, in the chaos of the day, I'd forgotten all about Tracy's request for six months off to travel around the world with her girlfriend. I didn't want to deny her the opportunity to experience the world with someone she loved, but could I handle running this place on my own for that long?

"How could I forget?" I said with a chuckle, trying to

steady my racing heartbeat. I was already feeling stressed with Nadia away, and now I had to consider running this place without Tracy for six months? Still, I didn't want to get in the way of her adorable relationship. "Let me look over the numbers for the next six months and make sure we can handle your absence, but... I don't see why you can't go." I cringed at the last words, but tried to hide them with a smile. I could think of a million reasons why Tracy shouldn't leave the inn for that long, but I didn't want to get into all of that with her right now.

"Awesome, thank you! I'll give Isabella a call right now and let her know the good news." Tracy pulled me into a hug, squeezing me tight, then practically skipped away from the front desk and back to her office as she called her girlfriend.

I sighed and focused on the computer screen in front of me. This would be fine. The Hemlock Inn practically ran itself sometimes. I could handle Tracy being gone for six months. And, in case things did go wrong, I'd make sure she only visited countries with cell service, so that I could call her when I needed help. Everything would be okay.

"Oh, thank goodness you're here!" Estelle burst through the inn's front doors, my mom trailing behind her. Fortunately, the lobby was empty, so no one heard this outburst. Lola poked her head up from behind the desk, quickly decided what was happening wasn't that interesting, and went back to sleep. Good to know that the scare with the chocolate bar earlier hadn't affected her ability to nap.

"Hey, what's going on?" I asked. "I didn't expect to see you back so soon. Everything okay?" I looked over at my mom for some indication of why she'd let Estelle leave her house when she needed to be grieving, but her face was hard to read.

"Kathleen was murdered!" Estelle cried out, her eyes wide and intense.

"Um, I'm sorry, what?" I asked, extremely confused about what was going on. "And can you please keep your voice down? We're not supposed to talk about what happened, remember?"

"Don't worry, the police told Kathleen's daughter already," Estelle said, waving her hand flippantly.

"They said Kathleen was murdered?" Oh, that poor woman.

"Well, no," Estelle said, some of the energy deflating out of her.

"But we found proof!" my mom interjected.

"And it's pretty serious," Estelle added.

My head spun as I looked between the two women. What exactly was going on here?

"Okay, I'm going to need you both to slow down," I said, holding my hands up to get them to calm down. "Start at the beginning. I thought the police said that Kathleen slipped and fell?"

"They did," Estelle said. "They claim she fell down her stairs, and that's how she died. But Kathleen was a dancer when she was younger. She was the most graceful person I'd ever met! No way did she slip and fall."

"But didn't you say so yourself, that she was getting old and not able to move around as much anymore? Isn't that why you were bringing her those cookies this morning?"

"But she was never unsteady on her feet. One of the reasons she stayed in a house with two stories was because she always knew she could handle the stairs. In fact, she took yoga classes twice a week! Does that sound like an old woman who can't use stairs every day? I mean, part of it was because the yoga instructor looked like Idris Elba and he'd always wear those short-shorts from the eighties, which she really liked, but still...Kathleen could do all the moves no problem. The only way she'd fall down her stairs was if someone pushed her!"

"Why would someone push her, though? She was a sweet old woman. What reason would someone have for killing her?"

"Well, that's what we need to figure out!" Estelle said, like it was the most obvious answer in the world. "I never liked her daughter very much. She lives in town with her husband, but she and Kathleen always had a volatile relationship. It stemmed from some fight between them years ago that they never resolved. Any time Kathleen talked about her, she'd say that Rebecca would ask her for money or get snippy with her and leave quickly. Rebecca was probably eyeing that big house that Kathleen lived in and just waiting for the day when she would inherit it. Maybe she finally decided that she couldn't wait any longer."

"So she killed her own mother? That seems like quite a stretch."

"It's not just that," my mom cut in. "We went by her house this afternoon. The police had finished their work, but her nurse was still around, cleaning up the room where... where it happened. I distracted her while Estelle took a look around the house, and the upstairs was in shambles! Blankets everywhere, paper all over the floor, and all of her beauty products strewn about the bathroom."

"So? Sometimes people are messy." I crossed my arms defensively, knowing that my living room was in a pretty similar state to how she'd described Kathleen's house.

"Not Kathleen!" Estelle said. "She was the neatest person I knew. Someone must've been looking around her house for something, and maybe Kathleen interrupted them, and so they pushed her down the stairs."

I pressed a hand against my forehead, taking a few deep breaths. I'd been concerned about Estelle since I had left her this morning, worried about how she was handling the loss of her friend. And now she was here, convinced that Kathleen had been murdered? Had she even had a chance to cry about what happened? Was she using the excuse of a potential murder as a way to keep her friend alive and not face the fact that she was gone?

"What do the police have to say about all this?" I asked after a moment.

Estelle scoffed. "Nothing! They claim Kathleen was an old woman who fell, even when I shared all this evidence. I called that Detective Patel down at the station, and all she'd say on the phone was that it was an accident and that she couldn't talk about it anymore. We need to find more proof if we're going to catch this killer!"

"*We* are not going to do anything," I said, waving my finger around to indicate the three of us. "You can't just go around claiming something is murder without any proof."

"Tell her what Miriam said, too," my mom piped up, and I glared at her. Now was not the time to egg on Estelle. She was like a dog with a bone when she became convinced of something—she just wouldn't let it go.

"Oh, that's right! I talked to Miriam, too," Estelle said, referring to her hairdresser's mother who worked down at the police station at the front desk and shared way more information than she should have. "She overheard the medical examiner discussing her report with one of the cops, and apparently her examination showed bruising around Kathleen's neck."

My eyes widened. "Really? And the police still don't think it was murder?"

"You know how incompetent that Chief Tate is. He's probably trying to cover it up so he doesn't have to investigate!"

I sighed. "Or bruising like that could have been caused by a fall, if she hit the wall on her way down. If the police don't think this was murder, I don't think we should go sticking our noses into things. I know Kathleen was a good friend of yours, but sometimes accidents just happen."

Estelle crossed her arms and furrowed her brow, like a petulant child. "I'm not wrong. I know this is murder, and if you won't do anything about it, then I will!"

I exhaled deeply, trying to keep my patience intact, and looked at my mom. "You're with her on this one?"

She shrugged. "Estelle raises some good points. It's at least worth looking into."

"Her nurse is pretty suspicious, too," Estelle added.

"That blonde woman who was at her house earlier? What makes you say that?"

"Kathleen kept telling me that she was always trying to get Kathleen to move into an old folks' home. Paula, that was her name, she said she was worried about Kathleen and thought she'd do better at a home. But Kathleen didn't need all that! She was so sprightly and graceful! Maybe she and Paula got into an argument about it, and Paula pushed her down the stairs."

"That's not a very good motive," I pointed out. "If Kathleen ended up at a nursing home, then Paula would be out of a job."

Estelle hesitated, unable to argue with my logic, then waved it away like a pesky bug. "No matter. Maybe it was her daughter, then. All I'm saying is that something suspicious is going on here, and we need to look into it."

"Estelle's right," my mom said. "Isn't it at least worth asking some questions? You two are good at this sleuthing thing, right?"

I never expected my mom to get caught up in Estelle's shenanigans like this. It was like I had another crime-obsessed Chrissy on my hands! Estelle was one of the most determined people I knew, and she wasn't going to let this go. As much as I wanted to stay out of all this, I couldn't let Estelle run around questioning people about a death that was likely an accident. Some people might be pretty upset about her insinuations—I knew that from my own experiences.

I couldn't let go of the feeling that Estelle was saying all of these things because she didn't want to admit that her friend was really and truly gone. Investigating her supposed murder gave Estelle a reason not to face the fact of Kathleen's death, and it would keep her busy. She wouldn't be able to move on with her life until she processed what had happened to Kathleen, and if she was so focused on finding a killer, she'd never slow down long enough to do that. I really didn't want to spend the last couple weeks of the year dealing with another death, but finding more proof that this was an accident might be the only way to help Estelle move on.

"All right, fine," I said after a moment of silence. "Let me talk to Detective Patel and see if I can get more information from her. I want to find out more about the bruising. But you need to promise that you'll stay here and stay out of trouble until I get back, okay?"

"Promise," Estelle said with a firm nod, her gaze steely. At least she wasn't crying anymore.

"I'll keep an eye on her," my mom said, already guiding Estelle back to the bistro.

I sighed and walked over to the front door, grabbing my jacket from the coatrack. The last thing I wanted to do right now was head out into the cold and go question a police detective about a death that likely wasn't even murder, but if this would help Estelle process Kathleen's death, then I had to help my friend.

5

Kathleen's death had rattled me this morning, and Estelle's claims that she'd been murdered had me concerned for how Estelle was handling her friend's death. While her evidence that Kathleen had been killed wasn't very strong, until we got a definitive answer, Estelle wasn't going to let this go.

Was it possible the police had found something at the crime scene that indicated more than just an accidental fall, an old woman unsteady on her feet? There was one place I could go to try to get some answers.

The Pine Brook Police Station was on the outskirts of town in a gray, short building. Rain slashed against my windshield as I drove, and I slowly turned into a parking spot once I got to the building, careful not to skid on the rain. At least it wasn't snowing right now.

I slipped on a raincoat as I dashed out of my car and shook off the raindrops while I stood in the front lobby. The police station lobby was drab and harshly lit, with a front desk running the length of one wall and a row of chairs across from the desk, next to the front door. Someone had managed to string up a strand of garland across the main wall of the lobby, though it drooped and was missing pinecones in places. A menorah was set up on a corner of the front desk, though no one had managed to light any of the candles yet.

The lobby was quiet as I entered, the only sound the tap of raindrops on the windows and the tapping of keys at the front desk. I smiled at Miriam as I walked over. The older woman was an excellent source of police information, and her insights had helped us crack more than one case in this town. She'd already revealed information about bruising to Estelle. If anyone was going to talk to me about what had really happened to Kathleen, it was her.

Before I had a chance to ask Miriam about Kathleen's death, one of the side doors burst open, and Chief Tate walked through, his face grumpy. He was a large man, with uniform shirts always a couple sizes too small and a face as red as a beet. His eyes narrowed as he saw me.

"What is she doing here?" he sneered, clearly assuming that I was unable to hear him across the ten-foot wide space.

"Oh, hello, Simone," Miriam said, looking up and smiling. "I'm not sure what she's doing here, Chief Tate, but I bet she'd tell you if you asked her."

I hid a smile as Tate turned his glare towards Miriam. It wasn't often that people talked back to Chief Tate, but Miriam was of the same mind as me: he was just a big bully with an impressive-sounding title and more aggression than brains.

I'd had my fair share of run-ins with Chief Tate, none of them all too pleasant. Normally, I'd run in the other direction if I saw him coming, especially since I'd been hoping to talk with Detective Patel instead, but since Kathleen's death was deemed an accident, he couldn't accuse me of trying to get involved in another murder investigation again. Honestly, all I was hoping for was confirmation that Kathleen's death was, in fact, an accident, so that I could tell Estelle and help her grieve her friend's passing.

"I'm looking for information about the death of Kathleen Richards. I understand you'd ruled it an accident; is that still the case?" I asked.

Tate's face managed to turn an even brighter shade of red. "You have no business coming here and asking about that poor woman's death. It was clearly an accident, and any suggestion to the contrary is hearsay!"

I was pretty sure that wasn't the definition of hearsay, but I didn't feel like correcting him in this moment. Tate wasn't likely to give me any useful information, but I'd rather soften him up so that he couldn't come up with some reason to toss me in a jail cell for the night.

"I still can't believe Mrs. Adler managed to call you so quickly," Tate grumbled. "The medical examiner hadn't even arrived to view the scene by the time you'd shown up at her house."

"I'm sorry, I didn't realize we were there so early. I don't mean to butt in, but you have to understand, Estelle and Kathleen were very close, and she's struggling with the news of her passing. She just had some questions about what happened to Kathleen."

"She's lucky I don't arrest her for disturbing the peace, going around and asking all these questions," Tate said, though his tone had softened with my apology. Like I thought, just a big bully who could be softened up with a placating tone.

"As I said, I don't mean to get in the way, but I'm trying to help Estelle process all of this. I know it was announced earlier that Kathleen had fallen, and that was what had killed her. Is that still the case? Was there any evidence that this may have been more than an accident?"

Apparently, that was the wrong question to ask, as Tate's face flushed red again, and he straightened up, looming over me. "Now, listen here, I will not have you go around making all sorts of false claims about the good people in this town. Kathleen Richards' death is tragic and a sad loss for Pine Brook, and it has nothing to do with you. You need to leave, now, before I make you."

My face reddened in embarrassment at his outburst, though my dark cheeks likely hid the flush. I glanced over at Miriam, who shrugged and sent me an apologetic look. I'd tried my best to reason with Chief Tate, but he was clearly not interested in listening to what I had to say. I didn't have to stand around, getting yelled at. I held up my hands in a placating gesture and backed out of the station, noticing Miriam picking up her phone and speaking into the line as I left.

Outside, I wrapped my jacket tighter around myself and dashed back to my car. Well, this had been a waste. I'd been looking for some official statement from the police about Kathleen's death so I could reassure Estelle that there wasn't anything nefarious going on, and instead I'd pissed off the police chief and was probably going to end up with a ticket for something I hadn't even done.

Once settled in my car, I pulled on my seatbelt and switched on the engine. Before I had a chance to pull out of my spot, however, the passenger door was yanked open and someone climbed into the car.

"Whoa, what are you doing?" I called out, jerking away from the passenger side.

"Calm down. I didn't think you'd want to have this conversation outside in the rain." Detective Monica Patel pulled down her hood and shook out her braid, splattering rain across my car. The tall Indian woman was who I'd come to the police station looking for, and it appeared she'd now found me.

"Miriam called you, didn't she?" I asked, remembering what the older woman had been doing on her phone as I was leaving the police station.

Patel nodded. "Why didn't you call me instead of coming to the station? You know Tate acts irrationally whenever you're around."

I shrugged. "I didn't think it'd be a big deal. He's not even around half the time anymore these days, is he? I don't know where he runs off to, but I figured he wouldn't notice that I was here."

"Well, you managed to pick the one day that he is around, and boy, was he upset when I passed him. You're going to need to stay away for at least a week if you don't want him to yell at you again."

I waved my hand flippantly, unconcerned. Chief Tate yelling at me wasn't the worst thing I'd had to deal with since coming to Pine Brook and, while I wasn't eager for it to happen again, I wasn't so scared.

"Thanks for coming out here. Did Miriam tell you why I came by?"

Patel nodded. "I'm sorry about Kathleen. I know you two were friends. How's Estelle handling it?"

"Not very well. In fact, she's convinced that Kathleen was murdered. She says that Kathleen was steady on her feet and never would've fallen like that."

"We looked into that. Kathleen was previously a ballerina dancer when she was younger, but she hadn't danced in years, and her nurse confirmed that she'd been more unsteady on her feet in recent months. My understanding is that Estelle and Kathleen spent most of their time playing cards together. Estelle wasn't likely to see Kathleen moving around too much on her feet."

"So it was an accident? You're sure about that?"

"Pretty sure. She likely died between ten P.M. and midnight, so she was probably getting ready for bed, or going to the bathroom, and slipped. This kind of thing happens, especially in a town like Pine Brook where the average citizen is retired. People get old, have trouble keeping their balance, and fall down. It's never fun, but I can guarantee it's not murder."

I let out a deep sigh. I hadn't realized how much I'd been hoping she would say that. While I was sad that Kathleen was gone, I didn't want Estelle to spend the rest of her days hunting for a killer that didn't exist. I could only now hope that Estelle would listen to me when I told her that I'd gotten that information from the police directly.

A thought flashed through my head, and I sat forward in my seat. "I heard there was bruising around Kathleen's neck. How do you explain that?"

Patel glared. "Where, exactly, did you hear that?"

"Um." I didn't want to tattle on Miriam and get her in trouble. "Estelle overheard one of the cops say something at the crime scene. Is it true?"

She let out an exasperated sigh. "Bruising can be common with a fall, especially if the person lost control as they went down. Stairs have a habit of leaving bruises all over the body."

I'd essentially told Estelle the same thing, that the bruising could've been from an accident, too. Maybe there wasn't anything suspicious going on here, after all.

"I'm sorry for all the questions. Just trying to help out my friend."

"I understand that, but you and Estelle need to stay out of this, okay?" Patel said, preparing to open her car door and leave. "I can't have you sticking your nose in where it doesn't belong."

"Wait—if it was an accident, what's there to stay out of? Does it really matter if Estelle asks questions about it?"

Patel paused, as if realizing what her words really meant. "I... Look, there's nothing to find here. I'm Head Detective now, and I can't talk about these sorts of things with civilians. There's nothing suspicious going on here, and Estelle shouldn't go around asking questions and bugging Kathleen's family while they're grieving. I have to go now." At that, she climbed out of my car and dashed into the police station.

I sat back in my seat after she'd left, thinking over what she'd said. Patel was convinced it was an accident, yet she didn't want Estelle asking more questions. Was that simply because she didn't want Estelle bothering Kathleen's family, or was it possible there was more going on that she wanted us to stay out of?

I didn't want to go back into the police station, in case Tate was still around looking to get into another fight, but Miriam still might've been able to help me out. I dialed her number at the station and quickly explained why I was calling.

"I'm not trying to make a mess for Kathleen's family or get in the way of anything, but Detective Patel made it seem like there might be more going on here than she originally let on. Do you know anything more about Kathleen's death?" I asked.

Miriam hesitated, going silent for so long I thought she'd hung up the phone. Then, finally, she spoke. "I shouldn't tell you this, but I liked Kathleen too, and I want to make sure the truth comes out... After Estelle mentioned that Kathleen used to be a dancer, Detective Patel had some extra tests run. I don't know what for—and the results haven't come back yet—but it's possible there's more going on here than Detective Patel officially said. I have to go now, bye." Miriam hung up quickly, leaving me sitting on an empty line with my mouth hanging open.

Why would Patel order extra tests if Kathleen's death was an accident?

6

"I knew it." Estelle's hands curled into tight fists. "Detective Patel must think she was killed."

"I don't know if we can go that far," I said, holding my hands out to calm down Estelle. We sat on the couches in the Hemlock's lobby with my mom, discussing what I'd learned at the police station.

I hadn't wanted to say anything to Estelle when I got back to the inn since Patel had warned me to stay out of this, but Estelle had pulled the information out of me. If Estelle was right about Kathleen being killed, and those tests proved it, then she deserved to know what was going on.

"We have to find the killer," Estelle went on. "If the police won't look into it properly, then we have to."

"But the police are looking into it," I reminded her. "Patel is running those tests."

"Who knows what those tests are for? Maybe she's just doing it because she has to when there's an accident. No, we need to find this killer and bring them to justice."

Had Estelle even spent any time today grieving her friend's death, or had she instead spent the whole day brainstorming how to catch a killer who might not even exist? Was she just using this as an excuse not to process her feelings?

"I know this is all really hard," I said gently, reaching out for Estelle's hand. "But I think we should leave this to the police. Have you even taken the time to grieve Kathleen's death?"

Estelle pulled away from me. "I'll grieve once her killer is behind bars."

"Won't you even consider looking into this?" my mom asked me. "You've found killers before, right? I don't want you getting into trouble, but if the police seem to think there's more going on here...maybe you can find some evidence to help them out."

I sighed and sat back in my seat, crossing my arms over my chest. I so didn't want to investigate another murder, especially not when the police were publicly claiming that it was an accident. But if I didn't do anything, then Estelle might go look for the killer alone, or, worse, with my mom tagging along, and I couldn't let that happen, either. I didn't want them getting into trouble.

"Look, we need to be careful about this. Either there's a killer out there, who won't appreciate us snooping around, or there isn't a killer, and the police will arrest us for meddling in Kathleen's affairs. Let me take the lead on this and see what I can find out. No snooping alone, okay?" I added sternly to Estelle.

"Promise!" she cried out, wrapping her arms around me. "Kathleen was a good woman, and she didn't deserve to die like this. She spent her whole life doing things for others: volunteering her time, lending a helping hand when someone needed it, encouraging folks in town to get to know each other so that we'd all feel closer...I need to honor her memory by finding the truth."

Tears pooled in my eyes at her words, and I discreetly wiped them away. I felt the same way about Estelle as she felt about Kathleen, and I couldn't imagine losing my friend so suddenly like this. Maybe finding some answers was the best way for Estelle to move on.

"I better go check on Miles and tell him what's happening," she added. She stood and hurried out of the inn.

A small ball of dread formed in the pit of my stomach as I watched her leave. As much as I wanted to help her process what happened to Kathleen, how quickly was I going to regret investigating an accidental death?

"I sure hope she's going to be okay," my mom said from beside me. "It's always hard losing a friend."

"I just hope she stays out of trouble." I let out a sigh and turned to my mom. "I should probably go check on things at the front desk. Are you going to be okay alone for a little while?"

"Of course! I know how to keep myself busy. You go do your work, and we'll catch up later. Bye-bye." She fluttered her fingers goodbye and then strode away towards the stairs.

The lobby was quiet, so I didn't actually need to rush off to the front desk, but I'd wanted a moment alone. I texted Nick, asking if he was free to chat. His reply was quick, and soon we were on the phone, where I explained what had happened with Kathleen.

"Oh, that's terrible. I'm so sorry to hear that. Are you okay?" he asked.

"I will be. I feel bad for Estelle. She and Kathleen were close, and she's not exactly taking this well."

"What do you mean?"

I hesitated. I hadn't mentioned Estelle's insistence that

Kathleen was murdered, and I wasn't quite ready to share this information with anyone else yet. While Nick never complained about my sleuthing, he didn't like me getting involved with murders, and he wouldn't be happy if he knew I'd agreed to help out Estelle. There was still a chance we wouldn't find any proof Kathleen had been murdered, so I didn't want to go around spreading rumors until I was more certain.

"Nothing," I said finally. "Just that she misses her friend, and she's having a hard time accepting what happened. She's with Miles now, so hopefully he can help ground her."

"He's always been good at that. Listen, I'm not sure if you already have plans, but I was talking to my dad about your mom's visit, and we'd love to have the two of you over for dinner tonight at the farm. What do you say?"

Maybe dinner with my boyfriend, his dad, and my mom was just what I needed to help me get over what happened to Kathleen. Of course, it also sounded like a potential recipe for disaster, but we were all adults, and my mom knew how to behave herself.

"That sounds great. Does seven work?"

"Perfect. See you then." We said our goodbyes and hung up, then I went in search of my mom to tell her about our plans.

"Oh, that sounds wonderful! I was hoping for a chance to get to know Nick better, and I'd love to meet Kenji. Seven works perfectly for me," she added with a grin.

"Great. Let's meet in the lobby then." I paused for a moment as something clicked into place in my head. "Wait a second...How did you know his dad's name was Kenji? I just said Nick and his dad wanted us over for dinner, but I never called him Kenji."

She blinked twice. "Really? Well, you must've said his

name sometime previously. Otherwise, how would I have known it?" She chuckled, guiding me to her room's door. "I was hoping to call your father and check in. I have no clue what time it is in Holland right now, but maybe he'll be awake. See you later!" She scooted me out the door before I had a chance to respond.

Shrugging, I headed downstairs to the lobby again. I probably had told her Nick's dad's name at some point in the past. It was a unique name—it must've stuck in her brain.

The rest of the day passed peacefully. A few guests checked in for the week, but for the most part, I got paperwork done at the front desk. Tracy was off at a few vendor meetings, and I spent the day mostly in silence, trying not to think too much about Kathleen's death, Estelle's determination to find her supposed killer, or Tracy's six-month vacation. Instead, I crunched numbers behind the desk and snuck Lola treats all day.

At six-thirty, my mom came down the stairs, bundled up in a raincoat and scarf. "The day just flew by! Do we still have enough time to get to the farm before dinner?" she asked, rubbing her hands together anxiously.

I nodded, typing a final key on the computer and then switching the machine off. "More than enough time. I need to stop at my apartment to drop off Lola, but that's in the same direction. Come on, let's go."

I hooked Lola up on her leash, and the three of us strolled out of the inn, out into the cold darkness. My mom chattered away about my dad's trip to Holland as I drove us through town, my hands tightening on the wheel. I'd managed to keep myself busy for most of the day, but now that we were heading to dinner, I was starting to get anxious. My mom was perfectly polite, and often very fun, but I didn't want anything to happen tonight that might cause tension between our families. My relationship with Nick was between the two of us, but if our parents didn't like each other, things could get awkward.

My mom followed Lola and me upstairs when we got to my apartment. "I'd just like to see how it looks!" she said when I pointed out that it'd be faster if she stayed in the car.

Once inside, I hurriedly set Lola up with a bowl of kibble and a chew stick, making sure the heat was on so she wouldn't get cold.

"Oh, dear, you need a Christmas tree," my mom said from the entryway, staring around the living room.

"Don't remind me." I pulled her back out of the apartment once I was finished with Lola and locked the door. "I haven't had time."

"Well, we'll have to add that to our list of things to do on our shopping trip," she said, looping her arm through mine as we headed downstairs and back to my car.

We made good time, pulling up to the farm just before seven P.M. I parked my car, and we dashed into the main barn, ducking our heads as rain started to fall. Nick's family farm was large, and employed a lot of people during the day. At night, the main barn was usually locked up, but lights blazed as we approached, and inside Kenji was setting plates out on a table against the far wall. The scent of miso soup and chicken skewers filled the air, and my stomach grumbled in anticipation.

My mom headed straight towards Kenji, waving enthusiastically, while my attention was caught by two people standing off to the side, near the front door. What was Hank doing here with Nick? I strode over, smiling as Nick looked up at my approach.

"Hey, fellas. What's going on? Hank, are you joining us

for dinner?" I didn't mind Nick inviting more people to our dinner, though it was a little weird to have one of my employees at dinner with my boyfriend, his dad, and my mom.

"Hey, Simone!" Hank's voice was louder than it needed to be, and his cheeks turned red as I came closer. He gripped a bundle of fabric in each hand. "I was just leaving." Before I had a chance to say anything more, he dashed past me and out of the barn.

"That was weird," I said with a chuckle, turning back to Nick. "What was that all about?"

Nick cleared his throat, shoving something blue into his pocket. "He-he was just checking on an order."

I furrowed my brow and snatched at the blue item Nick was hurriedly trying to put in his pocket. "Is that a tie? Is that what Hank was holding in his hands? Was he lending you a tie, or something?" I managed to snatch it out of his hands, curling my fingers around the fabric. It was actually a bow tie, and much nicer than something I'd expect Hank to own. He was always full of surprises, though.

Nick snatched it back, shoving it into his pocket and wrapping his arm around my shoulder to guide me towards our parents. "Sometimes we share ties. He's got good taste. I'm so glad to see you." He pulled me in for a kiss, causing me to put all thoughts of Hank and his fancy ties out of my head.

Kenji had gone all out for dinner, filling the table with platters of roasted, seasonal vegetables, fried dumplings, and enough soup to keep the chill outside from creeping inside. He pointed out the dishes he'd learned to make as a young boy from his father who'd grown up in Japan, and Nick explained how important it was for them to keep their

Japanese culture going now that they were so far from their ancestral home.

"Normally, Nick and I will have dinner together in the house, but when we have guests over, we like to get fancy in the barn. Makes it feel more like a party," Kenji explained, gesturing around the large space.

"This is so delicious," my mom said, digging into her rice bowl. "All I really know how to make is pancakes and frozen pizzas."

Kenji chuckled, taking a sip of wine. "We all have our strengths. I hear you're a fantastic doctor. That takes real skill and determination."

She brushed away the compliment, though her smile was wide. "It keeps me busy. It does feel good to know I'm helping the world, though, even in a small way. Growing food for people to eat is so important, too."

"We're pretty proud of it," Nick said, shooting a smile my way. We settled into our meals, the only sound the scrape of forks against plates and faint jazz music piped in from a speaker set up at the end of the table.

"Simone, I was so sorry to hear about what happened to Kathleen Richards," Kenji said, breaking the silence. "I understand you were close to her?"

I nodded, swallowing a bite of chicken skewer. "Not extremely close, but we were friendly. Estelle is taking it pretty hard, though. She and Kathleen were good friends. Kathleen was such a vibrant woman, and it's hard to think of her gone so suddenly." I kept to myself Estelle's suspicions about Kathleen being murdered, deciding it wasn't quite appropriate for the dinner table.

Kenji nodded. "Death comes for us all, but that doesn't make it any easier to deal with. I feel so lucky to have had such a long life, and I'm proud of the legacy I'll leave behind whenever it is my time to go. I hope Kathleen felt the same way in her final moments."

Tears pooled in my eyes, and I blinked them away, lowering my head. Kathleen had had a good life, and maybe it was finally her time to go. Still, I couldn't forget about the evidence Estelle had found indicating a more suspicious death. Was Estelle simply unable to accept the inevitability of death, or was there something more sinister going on?

7

Three days later, Estelle and I settled into a church pew. The black heels that I'd had to dig out of the back of my closet pinched my toes together, reminding me why I never wore these shoes. Other townspeople drifted into the church from the rainstorm outside. It was a dreary day for a funeral, but maybe that was the perfect kind of weather for an event like this. Maybe it would've felt weird to gather in response to Kathleen's death if it were bright and cheery outside.

She'd been a bright and cheery woman, though, so the rain clouds marking the sky didn't quite seem appropriate. A funeral at Christmas-time was always going to be sad, though, regardless of the weather. Had Kathleen been making plans for what she was going to do during the holiday before her death? She'd put up decorations around her house, which was more than I could say I'd done, so clearly she'd been looking forward to celebrating. And now, she'd never get the chance. My heart ached whenever I thought about her death.

I'd managed to keep Estelle on a short leash after I'd

decided to look into Kathleen's death. She'd agreed that it was wise for me to handle questioning people about what had happened since I'd had more experience grilling suspects in the past. Miles had also ended up needing more help with his hip, so Estelle had been busy with him the past couple of days. It was hard on her to see him in pain like this, even if she never told me as much. Caring for her husband, while also grieving the loss of her good friend, had caused Estelle to grow quieter over the past few days.

Fortunately, Miles was now feeling better, though not well enough to come out to Kathleen's funeral. Miles and Estelle lived in a single-story house, so at least I didn't have to worry about him tumbling down their stairs, but the front porch steps were still concerning. I was glad he was still taking things slow, even though his doctor had given him the all-clear to resume his normal activities. He'd decided to stay home, rather than potentially over-extend himself at Kathleen's funeral.

With Estelle busy with Miles and unable to pester me about Kathleen's death, my mom had also dropped her interest in the investigation, for which I was grateful. She'd been enjoying her time at the inn, spending hours at the spa or in the bistro, chatting up every guest or townsperson who crossed her path. I hadn't fully lost the tension in my shoulders over my anxiety about her visit, but every day was getting a bit easier.

The inn was fully booked, so I'd been kept on my toes trying to keep everything running, which meant my mom and I hadn't had time to go Christmas shopping for Nick yet. I still had a couple weeks until I needed to have the gift, but I kept reminding myself to plan a shopping trip with her before I ran out of time.

I had brought up Sylvia's letter once again, but Mom

hadn't been interested in talking about it. In fact, she changed the topic as soon as I mentioned it, as if I hadn't said anything in the first place. I still wanted to know what issue Sylvia had been referring to in her letter, what reason there had been for their estrangement all those years, but a part of me also wondered if I should just drop the whole thing.

I'd never been very good about confronting my mom about these types of things. Once, a few years ago, back in Los Angeles, she'd randomly shown up at my apartment one evening, announcing that she was spending the night with me—not unlike what she'd done on this trip. That time, however, it was clear she was upset about something, and I had a feeling it had had to do with my dad. My mom's birthday had been the week before, and my dad didn't have a great track record of thoughtful birthday presents.

Even knowing that she was likely upset with my dad, I'd still tiptoed around the issue and been unable to straight-up ask her what was going on. It had taken a desperate call to Chrissy to resolve the issue, as Chrissy had then shown up the next day and practically demanded that my mom go back home and work things out with Dad. She left my apartment that same day. Chrissy had always been better at getting straight to the point than me.

It felt like the same kind of situation was happening all over again, where I knew there was more to the story. In fact, I had Sylvia's written words to prove that there was more to it, but I was incapable of confronting my mom with the truth. Since I didn't think Chrissy would want to fly all the way out here from Hawaii to save my butt again, my strategy was to do nothing and hope that my mom would open up to me on her own. I wasn't holding my breath on this one.

Though I was busy with the inn, I couldn't help myself

from thinking about the bruising Miriam had told us about, and the extra tests that Detective Patel was running. What could they mean? Had someone killed Kathleen and tried to make it look like an accident? According to the police, Kathleen's death was accidental—at least, that was what they'd told the local newspaper. Still, was there something else going on?

The church pews around us filled up with other guests, all in black, and a man in a long robe came out through a door in the front of the room, approaching the pulpit. He opened a small black Bible and began reading from the pages. I've never spent much time at church, and as the man's monotonous voice filled the cavernous room around us, I had to wonder if this was the kind of vibe Kathleen actually wanted for her funeral. Given her vibrant nature, I'd expected something less sober.

After the pastor finished his reading, a woman approached the pulpit, clutching a small, white notepad. She set her notepad down and cleared her throat, the microphone in front of her picking up the sound and amplifying it throughout the church. She gripped the sides of the pulpit and took a deep breath.

She was a short woman, with brown hair pulled back into a low bun and pale skin that seemed translucent from this far away. Her simple black dress had a high neckline and long sleeves that pooled around her wrists. A gold band shone from her ring finger.

"Thank you all so much for coming to my mother's funeral," she said, her voice starting out low and small, then gradually gaining momentum as she spoke. "I know she would be grateful to see you all here. I'd like to read a short passage from Ralph Waldo Emerson, as remembrance for my mother."

She began reading from her notepad, her voice filling the room around us and giving me a chance to study her. So this was Kathleen's daughter, Rebecca. After all I'd heard about her from others, I'd expected...more. A louder voice, a bigger personality... Not this tiny mouse of a woman. Kathleen had been such a lively, spirited woman, I'd expected the same from her daughter. Of course, this was also a woman who had just lost her mother and was dealing with all the stress that came with that. Maybe I should cut her more of a break.

I tilted my head to the side as she continued reading. Did she look like a killer? In all honesty, she looked like a big gust of wind could potentially knock her over, but I'd seen killers smaller than her. Anything was possible, especially where money was involved. I wasn't going to get a good impression of the kind of person that Kathleen's daughter was from this far away, so I'd need to find another way to get closer to her.

Before we'd entered the church, Estelle had given me a rundown on Kathleen's daughter and son-in-law. "She's nice enough, although she and Kathleen have never been very close. I'm not really sure why. Kathleen never much liked her husband, David. She never told me why—I don't think she liked talking badly about them—but I always noticed tension whenever she would mention him. We should try to see if we can talk to Rebecca to learn more about what happened to Kathleen."

In the church, I strained my neck to the side to see if I could spot Rebecca's husband up at the front, but all I managed to do was bump into the woman sitting next to me. Mouthing my apologies and ignoring her glare, I settled back into my seat, hands in my lap. Rebecca announced that there would be a receiving line once the service was finished, which would hopefully give me a chance to question her more and talk to her husband.

Estelle sniffled from beside me, tears rolling down her cheeks. I gently grabbed her hand and squeezed, feeling my eyes pool with tears. A woman sitting next to Estelle passed us each a tissue, smiling sadly, and the three of us quietly watched Rebecca continue her poem, tears now flowing freely.

While I wanted to gain more information about Kathleen's life to determine what really happened to her, even I wasn't heartless enough to make it through a funeral with a dry eye. After Rebecca finished her poem, a few more people filed up to the pulpit and said some words about Kathleen, sniffles and sobs coming from the crowd.

Once the funeral was finished, Rebecca announced the receiving line would begin, and I turned to Estelle, my hand still holding hers. Though she'd been interested in speaking with Rebecca about Kathleen when we first arrived, she most definitely didn't look up for questioning any suspects now. As determined as she was to find evidence of a killer, it was clear Kathleen's funeral had overwhelmed her.

"Are you okay?" I asked, keeping my voice low.

Estelle nodded, wiping at her tears with a tissue. "I think I'd like to leave now."

"Of course." I hesitated a moment, debating the merits of what I was about to say. We could just leave and continue grieving Kathleen somewhere else, but I knew Estelle's determination to figure out what really happened to her friend would eventually return, and she might be even more upset that we lost out on a chance to speak with Rebecca. As much as I hated the idea of questioning a grieving daughter, I wanted to keep Estelle from doing it herself if I could. "I'd still like to speak with Rebecca, see if she might know anything about her mother's death. Do you want to wait in the car while I do that?"

Estelle's eyes sparkled as she looked up at me, whether from tears or the reminder that we were snooping to find a killer, one of her favorite activities, I couldn't be certain. "Take all the time you need. I'll be waiting for you outside." She patted my hand one last time, then stood and joined the line of people exiting our row.

I stayed in my seat for a few minutes longer, letting the crowd clear out before I made my move. I wanted to catch Rebecca at the end, when most people were already gone and when she might be more likely to open up about her mother. I'd been told by different people that there was some tension between Kathleen and Rebecca, and I wanted to see what I could find out.

Finally, I went to join the receiving line, brushing a lock of curly hair that had escaped my bun back into place. Rebecca was greeting guests with a man at her side, presumably her husband. He was tall and wide, like a linebacker, and it wasn't hard to imagine him overpowering Kathleen and pushing her down those stairs. Oh man, I really hoped this had just been an accident, as the idea of someone intentionally hurting someone as kind and energetic as Kathleen was almost too much to bear.

I made it to the front of the line and held out my hand with a smile. "I'm so sorry for your loss. Your mom was a wonderful woman. My name is Simone. I own the Hemlock Inn."

Rebecca's gaze softened. "Oh, you must know Estelle, right? I didn't see her in the crowd."

"She left after the service. She's a little upset, as I'm sure you can imagine."

"She sent along some flowers, which was very sweet of

her. I wanted to thank her for them. She and my mother were close. I can only imagine what she's going through right now."

"She feels the same about you, of course. Losing a parent is never easy, is it?"

"No, it isn't. But it happens, of course, especially as you get older."

Rebecca's husband David shifted beside her, tugging at his tie, but I kept my eyes on her. "It must be so hard for this to have happened so suddenly. I know Kathleen was older, but she always seemed so sprightly when I saw her around town. It's hard to believe that she could slip like that."

Rebecca shrugged. "It just kind of happens as you get older. My mom was getting slower in her older years, too. She'd had a nurse with her, who's been such a great help. She actually offered to stay onboard and help us pack up the house, which is so thoughtful of her. I'm not sure if I'd be able to take care of it all without the extra help."

"That is considerate of her. It's good to know that Kathleen had someone around to help her out as she got older." I also made a mental note to see what else I could learn about this nurse.

Rebecca nodded. "She was helpful, but as my mom got older, I was considering maybe putting her in a nursing home soon. I have to wonder if having more constant care might've prevented something like this from happening." At those words, her eyes filled with tears, and she lowered her head into a handkerchief, wiping at her face.

"All of this must be so tough for you," I said after a couple of moments, once Rebecca had gotten her tears under control. "I can't even imagine all the work you have to do when someone passes away like this. Kathleen owned her house in town, right? Are you planning on selling it?"

"Well, I'm not so sure about that," Rebecca said, twisting her handkerchief between her fingers.

David leaned in and interrupted our conversation. "Yes, we will be selling it. Let us know if you happen to know any real estate agents."

I jerked back in surprise as his large frame crowded the space. "I'll keep that in mind. I, um, I've seen her house before. It's beautiful. I'm sure you'll get a lot of money for it."

David pursed his lips and sneered. "We're not worried about that. We just want to make sure it's taken care of."

"Of course," I said with a casual wave of my hand. "Finding a good real estate agent will help with that, I'm sure. What sorts of things did Kathleen enjoy doing in the weeks before her death? Was she active? Did she spend much time with you?"

Rebecca narrowed her eyes. "Things were pretty normal before her death. It's what makes this so tragic. What's with these questions?"

"No particular reason. I'm just trying to get to know Kathleen a bit more." I kept my face neutral, hoping not to set her off. It didn't seem to work.

Rebecca leaned forward, wagging her finger in my face like a school teacher. "I know what this is. I know about you and all your snooping around town, looking for murderers. I can't believe you would come here and suggest anything of the sort. My mother died tragically, and there was nothing suspicious about it. I think it's best if you leave now."

I took a step back and held my hands up in a placating gesture. "I'm sorry for intruding like this. Like I said, I'm just trying to learn what I can about Kathleen."

"And I said you need to leave." Rebecca took a step closer to me and jabbed her finger at me, lifting her wrist. As she did, her dress sleeve slipped down her wrist, and dark spots appeared on her skin. She gave a squeak and slapped her other hand over her wrist, covering up the dark spots. "I-I need to go," she stammered, glancing around like a trapped animal. She turned on her heel and dashed out of the room, David hurrying after her.

Yikes, now I'd managed to scare off a grieving daughter. Why did I have to always go around asking people these ridiculous questions? I was trying to help find the truth for Estelle, but sometimes it felt like I just made things worse for people.

And what had been all over her wrist? Was Rebecca sick? Or were those bruises?

A few of the other guests glared at me once Rebecca and David were gone. I quickly dashed out of the church, keeping my gaze down. Clearly, I wasn't welcome here anymore.

8

The rain had stopped falling outside the church, but there was a chill in the air, and I was glad I'd grabbed my coat before leaving. Estelle should've been keeping herself warm in my car, and I hoped she'd had a chance to process her feelings about what had happened with Kathleen, particularly after all the emotions she'd felt at the funeral. However, she was so convinced that Kathleen had been murdered, I didn't know if she'd feel any better until Kathleen's killer was caught. If Kathleen hadn't been murdered, and there was no killer to catch, would Estelle be able to move on from all of this? Or would she spend the rest of her days hunting for a killer that didn't exist?

I wrapped my arms around myself as I stood on the church steps. I felt like a real jerk for making Rebecca so upset inside. I'd thought I'd done a good job of keeping my questions vague and nonspecific, but she was smart and she'd seen right through me. Suggesting that her mother had been killed was a serious thing, so it was reasonable that she'd get upset.

However, was her reaction over the top? If Kathleen had been killed, wouldn't Rebecca want to know the truth? Unless, of course, she and her bully of a husband had something to do with Kathleen's death. There was no evidence of that, but her reaction in the church had seemed possibly over the top.

What did I know, though? Grief could make people do things they wouldn't normally, and I didn't want to assume that Rebecca was a killer simply because she'd gotten upset at me for asking all these questions at her mother's funeral.

Just then, Estelle came up the stairs and reached out for me. "I heard loud voices coming from inside the church. Is everything okay?"

"I thought you were going back to my car?" I pulled her into a hug, wrapping my arms around her tight. It was too chilly for Estelle to be standing outside alone like this.

"I wasn't quite ready to go back to your car yet. I wanted a moment to myself out here. Did you learn anything from Rebecca?"

I shrugged. "I'm not really sure. She didn't like me asking all those questions, but I probably wouldn't like it, either, at my mother's funeral."

Something grabbed Estelle's attention over my shoulder, and she stood on her tiptoes and waved her hand in the air. "Louise! Over here!" Turning to me and lowering her voice, she added, "Louise and Kathleen played bridge together for years. Maybe she knows something about Kathleen's death."

A woman wearing an oversized raincoat approached us and pulled Estelle into a hug. She was older, probably in her mid-seventies, with curly white hair sprouting out from her head. She smiled, her eyes crinkling in the corners, as she turned to me.

"My name is Louise," she said, holding out her hand to

shake. "You're Simone, isn't that right? I've seen you around town. I was so sad to learn that Sylvia had passed away, but it seems like you've done a great job at the inn. That bistro of yours is truly magnificent."

"Well, I'm glad you like it," I said, shaking her hand. "I'd like to think Aunt Sylvia would be proud of what I'd done with the place."

"I'm sure she would be. I didn't realize you knew Kathleen."

"I did, a bit. I'm closer to Estelle here, but I met Kathleen a few times through her."

"Was that you who got into that argument with Rebecca inside?" she asked, gesturing over her shoulder towards the church.

I hung my head, ashamed, and nodded. "Yes, that was me. I'm so embarrassed, I never expected that kind of reaction."

"Well, grief can make people do strange things," Louise said, crossing her arms over her chest.

"Louise, do you mind if we talk to you about Kathleen? We're looking into the circumstances surrounding her death," Estelle said.

Louise's eyes widened. "Oh, dear. What do you think happened?"

"That's what we'd like to talk to you about. Why don't we step over here?" She led Louise down the steps and around to the side of the church, where there was a small gazebo and a few chairs set out, protected from the rain.

I sighed and followed after them. I didn't know why we needed to question this random friend of Kathleen's, but Estelle was determined and I didn't know how to politely stop her from what she was doing.

Once we were settled under the gazebo, Estelle turned to

me. "Simone, didn't you have some questions?"

I tried not to roll my eyes at this switch around. Of course, now Estelle wanted me to take the lead on this one. I plastered on a smile and turned to Louise, figuring maybe she'd have something useful to share. "How long did you know Kathleen?"

"Oh, for years," Louise said. "We were in the same grade in school. We both left Pine Brook to go to college, but returned not long after once we were married. We connected again pretty soon after. My husband passed away about ten years ago, and Kathleen's husband ran off when Rebecca was just a baby. But we still managed to bond. We played bridge together throughout the years. Recently, Kathleen was less up for the game, though I'd still stop by her house on a regular basis to check in. I always wanted to make sure she was okay, especially since she was all alone in that house. I moved to a retirement community a few years ago, so I'm never really alone. But I know Kathleen loved her independence and never wanted to leave that house."

"Were Rebecca and her mother close?"

Louise shrugged. "Off and on, over the years. Kathleen never much cared for Rebecca's husband, David, but she didn't want to do anything to make their relationship worse, so she didn't say much about it. I think Kathleen was worried in recent months that Rebecca was going to try to put her in a nursing home. That was the worst thing, in Kathleen's opinion, but I told her it probably wasn't as bad as she thought."

Rebecca had admitted she was considering a nursing home for her mother. Was she trying to get Kathleen out of her house and into a home so that she could sell her mother's house? If Kathleen didn't want to move, Rebecca wouldn't have much of a chance of getting at her house, but now that Kathleen was dead, that option opened back up for her.

"I'm sure all this must be hard for you, and I don't mean to make any assumptions, but part of me wonders if Kathleen's fall was really an accident."

Louise cocked her head to the side. "What do you mean?"

"Well, Estelle keeps saying that Kathleen was really confident on her feet. She used to be a dancer, right? And she took a lot of yoga classes? It's hard to believe that she'd fall like this, given how steady she was on her feet."

Louise furrowed her brow. "Yes, it's true Kathleen was a dancer, and she still kept up her yoga routine, but she was also getting old. Even the most sure-footed person can only win out against the Grim Reaper for so long. At some point, he finds us all..." Louise's voice trailed off and she stared into the distance.

I shifted in my seat, glancing up at Estelle, who motioned for me to keep going. "I'm sorry for even suggesting something like that could happen, but I told Estelle I would look into it. Does any of this sound reasonable to you? Can you think of any reason why someone would want to hurt Kathleen?"

"Well, I..." Louise started, but her cheeks turned pink and she snapped her mouth shut.

"What? What is it? Do you know something?"

"No, I, I mean, I shouldn't have said anything." She got flustered and started messing with the zipper on her raincoat, fiddling with her purse, just generally seeming very nervous.

"Louise, it's okay. You can talk to us about what's going on." Estelle reached out to squeeze the other woman's hand, but Louise slipped out of her grasp and stood.

"I should go. I, um, I have somewhere to be." Without another word, she dashed away from the gazebo and towards the parking lot.

"Whoa, what was that about?" Estelle asked as we watched Louise flee.

"I don't know," I said, thinking back over our conversation. "I don't think I said anything all that bad to set her off like that. Jeez, why am I even doing this? That's the second person in less than an hour that I've managed to upset with all my questions about Kathleen."

"All this means is that Kathleen must've been killed," Estelle said. "Otherwise, why would everyone be acting so weird around us? I've known Louise for a few years, and she's not normally like that."

"You can't really believe that Louise had anything to do with Kathleen's death, though, can you? She seemed like such a nice woman."

"No, you're probably right. But maybe she knows something about who did do it. Maybe she realized something about Rebecca or David, and that's why she had to leave so quickly. She didn't want anyone to know that she has proof that they killed Kathleen."

"Okay, now that's really a stretch," I said, holding my hand up to keep her from going on. "Maybe we just scared off an old woman at her good friend's funeral. Ever think about that?"

Estelle crossed her arms and shook her head, looking quite like a petulant child. "No, there's definitely more going on here, and we need to find the truth for Kathleen's sake.

Louise was holding something back, and Rebecca definitely has her secrets. We can't stop digging."

I sighed and pressed my hand against my temple. Investigating an accidental death and looking for a murderer was starting to give me a headache.

"Are you sure you aren't seeing more here than there really is? It's always hard to lose a friend. Is it possible you're seeing a murder where there isn't one because you're having trouble accepting what happened to Kathleen?" I tried to keep my voice gentle, not wanting to set Estelle off, but she still tensed beside me.

She paused for a moment, then her voice was determined and steady. "No, that's not what's happening here. There's a killer running loose, and since the police aren't interested in looking, we need to find them."

"Well, what do you suggest we do now? I don't think any of those people are going to talk to us again."

"Go back to the scene of the crime. Check out her house. Maybe there's something we missed before."

I let out a deep breath and stood. "All right, I'll see what I can find out. But you need to go home and check on your husband, okay? I'll give you a lift back into town."

Estelle hurried after me as I strode to my car. "What about those bruises Miriam told us about? What did the police have to say when you asked?"

"Um, Detective Patel just kept saying it was an accident. Maybe Miriam was wrong about the bruising." I thought back to when Detective Patel had told me to stay away from Kathleen's death. Why would she do that if there wasn't anything to investigate? I didn't want to encourage Estelle any more than I already was, so I kept that thought to myself.

"Hmm. I'll talk to her again to see what I can find out."

I held in a groan as we climbed into my car, Estelle continuing to discuss different motives. All of this snooping around was quickly turning into a very bad idea, based on the number of people I was upsetting.

9

After Kathleen's funeral, Estelle was even more convinced that there was something suspicious going on with her death. While I didn't want there to be another killer running around Pine Brook, I had to agree that we'd met some interesting characters at her funeral. Kathleen's daughter and son-in-law had quickly gotten aggressive with me—though could you blame them given the questions I'd been asking? Still, had that quick turn to anger come up when talking with Kathleen at some point, and resulted in a push down her stairs?

And then there was Kathleen's supposed friend, Louise. I didn't want to assume the worst of her, as she seemed like a genuinely nice woman, but her sudden departure from the funeral had been suspicious. Was she simply a kind person, grieving the loss of her friend? Or did she have some secret that could explain what had happened to Kathleen?

I hadn't spotted Kathleen's nurse at the funeral, which made sense. Paula was an employee of the family and probably had other clients she had to deal with during the day. However, she'd spent the most time with Kathleen leading up to her death, so I wanted the chance to talk to her and see what information she could share. Kathleen's daughter had told me that Paula was still helping out around Kathleen's house after her death. I didn't know why her nurse would stick around when her client had passed away, but it made my job easier if Paula was at Kathleen's house.

It gave me an opportunity to kill two birds with one stone since there was also the fact that Estelle and my mother had seen Kathleen's house in shambles after her death. According to Estelle, Kathleen was a tidy woman who wouldn't have wanted her house to get like that. Was the mess some indication that something nefarious had been going on in that house? Only one way to find out.

The morning after Kathleen's funeral, I woke to rain pattering against my windows. I took in a deep breath and stared up at the ceiling. It was hard enough to imagine that Kathleen was dead, and now there was the possibility that she'd been killed. I'd hoped to be away from any killers for the holiday season, but if my mother and Estelle were to be believed, that wasn't going to be the case.

I was more interested in heading up to my boyfriend's apartment and spending the rest of the morning with him, rather than running outside into the rain on the trail of a potential killer, but I'd given my word to Estelle the day before. I had to help find justice for Kathleen, however I could.

I hopped out of bed and had a quick shower, then took Lola on a walk around the block. She didn't appreciate the rain splashing on her head as we walked. I rubbed her down with a towel when we returned, then settled her back on her dog bed with a chew stick. She'd be content here for a few hours without me, but I'd make sure to swing by and take her to the inn after I'd finished snooping around Kathleen's house and talking with her nurse.

My lack of decorations in my apartment seemed particularly noticeable this morning, given how dreary it was outside, and how much I didn't want to go around questioning people about a poor woman's death. I needed to get a Christmas tree or some twinkling lights or something if I was going to keep my spirits up this season.

Rain splashed against my windshield as I drove through town, and I turned the heater up to high, shivering in my seat. Snow wasn't expected in the forecast for several weeks, likely not even until January, but the temperatures were surely heading in that direction.

I drove slowly, not wanting to get into trouble while in my car, and made it to Kathleen's house in good time. I pulled in across from Kathleen's house, peering out the window to see if there was any movement. Too much rain poured down from the sky, and I had trouble seeing much of anything. I sighed and wrapped my raincoat around myself. Only one way to see what was going on.

I dashed out of my car and hurried up to Kathleen's front porch. Fortunately, she had an overhang which kept the porch mostly dry, so hopefully my curly hair wouldn't get soaked and drip water down my back all day. Unfortunately for me, the rain was beginning to turn horizontal, and I wouldn't be safe out here for much longer. I knocked on the door three times, my teeth chattering. Would anyone be home? Or was I stuck out here in the rain for the foreseeable future?

After a moment, the door swung open, and a tall blonde woman wearing pink scrubs stood on the other side. She was the same woman I'd spotted at Kathleen's house on the day she'd died. This woman, presumably Paula, furrowed her brow in concern when she saw me, and she stepped to the side, waving me in.

"Come in, come in," she said, practically grabbing my arm and yanking me inside. "Can't have you catching a cold like that out there, now can we?"

"Thanks," I said, slipping out of my rain coat and passing it to her so that she could hang it from a hook. Rather than drenching the whole house, my soaking coat was now restricted to one section of the entryway. "I'm so sorry to intrude like this. I wasn't sure if anyone would be here."

"Not at all." The woman waved away my concerns with a flick of her wrist. "I'm Kathleen's nurse. Well, I suppose I *was* her nurse, now. I know it seems a little weird to still be here after Kathleen has passed away, but I've already been paid through the end of the month, and I wanted to help Rebecca out. I'm mostly sorting and organizing things, so Rebecca can figure out what she wants to save, and I'm trying to clear out the kitchen to donate the perishables. I got a little caught up in reminiscing about dear Kathleen, and the whole morning got away from me. I still need to dust the curtains before I leave. Would you like some tea? I just put on the kettle."

"That would be wonderful," I said, rubbing my hands together to warm them up and following this woman into the kitchen. "I'm so sorry for your loss. It's kind of you to offer to help Rebecca out."

"Thank you, dear," she called over her shoulder, heading towards the stove to grab the kettle that had started shrieking as we'd entered the kitchen. "My mother passed away a few years ago, so I know how hard it is to pack up a parent's house. I wanted to do what I could to help make things easier for Rebecca. The name's Paula. You're Simone, right? From the Hemlock Inn?"

I nodded, not surprised she knew who I was. Pine Brook was a small town, and local business owners were usually well-known. Plus, with the addition of the spa and the continued use of the bistro, lots of town residents spent more time at the inn than ever before. "I wasn't extremely close to Kathleen, but we were friends. I thought I'd come by to see if Rebecca needed help with anything. I was so sad to hear the news of Kathleen's passing."

"Yes, it's quite a tragedy," Paula said, pulling two mugs down from the cupboard. "Chamomile okay? I can't have anything with caffeine past ten A.M., or else I'm up half the night."

"That would be great. Anything to chase out this chill."

"I know, it's so awful out there right now. I heard on the news we may get some snow. While I'm not eager to shovel out my driveway, it's got to be better than this bitter rain."

"Tell me about it. How are you holding up with everything?"

Paula shrugged, pouring hot tea into the mugs and passing one across to me. She took a sip of hers before she spoke. "In my line of work, your clients don't always last that long. It's not the first time I've had to deal with death. Kathleen was different, of course. Such a sweet, kind woman, with one of the best senses of humor in the state. But she was getting up there in years. I'd have been surprised if her daughter didn't put her in a home in the next couple of months."

"Really?" I took a sip of my tea to give myself a moment to compose my thoughts. "Kathleen always seemed so independent. I imagine she wouldn't have been too happy with that turn of events."

"It's one of the toughest conversations a child has to have with a parent, that's for sure. Kathleen wouldn't have appreciated the suggestion at first, but she would've come around to it eventually. She was starting to understand that things were taking a turn, and there was only so much I could do since I wasn't here all the time."

"I thought Kathleen went to a yoga class every week? Wouldn't that have kept her active and sprightly?"

"She did take a weekly yoga class, but there are different types of yoga, and I don't think she did the more intensive kind. She definitely wasn't as active as she used to be."

"Were you here when it happened? Sorry, I don't mean to pry," I added hurriedly, realizing how callous the question was, plus I'd seen Paula at the house when I'd come by to get Estelle. Still, I wanted to hear from Paula how she was involved in all of this. "It's just, you were so close to Kathleen. Were you with her most days?"

Paula nodded. "I was the one who found her on that day, and I was around most days. Rebecca had increased my hours so I could spend more time with her mother. But I couldn't be here all the time—it was too expensive for them."

I murmured something non-committal, staring down into the depths of my tea. Had Rebecca considered having Kathleen move in with her? If Kathleen's illness had progressed so much, Rebecca may not have been able to do anything for her, either. A nursing home might've been the best option. Was it really that surprising that she'd have issues navigating her stairs? But did a fall down the stairs really explain the bruising around her neck, or the extra tests Detective Patel was running?

"This must look awful," Paula said suddenly, pulling my attention back to her. "Me, here, claiming to be packing up the house, and instead drinking from Kathleen's mugs. It's just so strange—I spent so much time in this kitchen with Kathleen, it feels normal to make myself some tea and chat with a friend. With Kathleen gone, I'm not only out of a job, but I've lost an important person, too." Her eyes filled with tears, and she pressed her hand against her eyes, taking a deep, shuddering breath.

I stood and glanced around the kitchen, snatching a tissue from a box on the counter. I passed it to Paula and patted her shoulder gently. "I can only imagine how tough this must be for you. I know I'd get attached to my patients after spending so much time with them. Kathleen was a wonderful woman."

"Yes, she truly was." Paula wiped at her eyes and blew her nose on the tissue, then took another sip of her tea. "She's not my only client, of course, but she was the one that I spent the most time with in the past few months. I'll have to find some way to replace that income with a new patient, but it's not an easy field to be in. Sometimes families would rather just chuck their elderly parents off to a nursing home, rather than letting them stay in their homes with the help of a nurse."

"How do you find your patients? Do you have connections in town?"

She shook her head. "I'm contracted through an agency that helps me find new clients. The Hawthorne Nursing Group in Holliston. It's a network of nurses throughout the Pacific Northwest. I've got a few contacts in the group who might be able to help connect me with new patients, but the pool of potential clients is rather small. Everything is so expensive these days, it can be hard for families to afford the extra cost of in-home help."

Kathleen at least had been able to maintain her independence, so well that I didn't even know she'd had an in-home nurse until now. Given her vibrancy about life, I wasn't surprised that she'd been able to stay out of a nursing home for so long.

"Do you know much about Kathleen's relationship with Rebecca?" I asked. "I've heard things were strained between them."

Paula swiped at the tears under her eyes and tilted her chin in thought. "They weren't extremely close, it's true. I don't know what happened between them, but Kathleen was always sad that they weren't closer. Actually..." Paula's voice trailed off, her gaze down.

I straightened up at her words. What wasn't she saying? "Sorry, I don't mean to ask all these questions. I'm just curious about Kathleen's life. Plus, I'm trying to help out my friend, Estelle Adler—maybe you know her? She was close with Kathleen."

Paula smiled faintly. "Ah, yes, I know Estelle. This must be so tough for her."

"Yes, she's having a hard time accepting Kathleen's death, and I'm just trying to understand more about what happened to her, to bring Estelle some closure. At Kathleen's funeral yesterday, I got the sense from Rebecca that they weren't close. But that happens with mothers and daughters sometimes, right?"

Paula nodded, running her finger up and down the side of her mug. "It's true, that can happen sometimes. Honestly, I wouldn't have been surprised to learn that Rebecca wanted to put Kathleen up in a nursing home. Like I said, a daily nurse is expensive, and I know Rebecca and David believed they could get a lot of money selling this house. I always thought he seemed a bit too excited about the prospect of selling this house. And now, I guess that's what'll happen..."

Her voice trailed off again, and we sat in silence for a few moments.

"Do you mind if I use the bathroom?" I asked, breaking the silence.

Paula straightened up, pulled out of her reverie about Kathleen and her daughter. "Of course, no problem at all. It's down the hallway, two doors down."

"Thank you." I smiled and stood, exiting the kitchen while she continued drinking her tea.

This insight from Paula was useful, but I didn't want to ask too many more questions and make her more suspicious about why I was curious. If Paula had killed Kathleen, which didn't seem likely given how upset she seemed about Kathleen's death, I didn't want her to realize that I thought Kathleen's death was anything but accidental. Still, I had some more questions about Kathleen's relationship with her daughter, and what would happen to Kathleen's house now that she was dead.

I strode down the hallway towards the bathroom, poking my head into a few rooms as I passed. Living room, dining room, stairs leading up to the second floor. I glanced over my shoulder to make sure Paula wasn't watching, then switched on the faucet in the bathroom to make it seem like I was using it. I shut the bathroom door, then scurried up the stairs, keeping my feet light.

So far, I hadn't seen any of the shambles that Estelle and my mother had reported on earlier in the week. In fact, Kathleen's house looked very clean. On the second floor, I poked my head into a few bedrooms and an office, but everything looked spic-and-span. Had Estelle and my mom been wrong about the mess they'd seen, or had Paula had a chance to clean things up since Kathleen died? Paula did say that was more or less why she was here, to get things organized for Rebecca to go through, so maybe it wasn't surprising.

Snooping around a dead woman's house wasn't making me feel all that good inside, so after checking the last two rooms, I went back downstairs and stopped off at the bathroom, flushing the toilet and walking out like I'd just finished washing my hands. Paula was still in the kitchen when I returned, rinsing off her mug at the sink.

"Thank you so much for chatting with me," I said as I entered the kitchen, picking up my mug and bringing it over to the sink. "I'm glad Kathleen had someone in her life that's able to help her out now that she's gone."

"Thanks for stopping by. Stay dry out there, okay?" Paula sent me another smile, then she led me through the house and out the front door.

Once outside, I turned towards the street, wrapping my jacket tighter around myself. The rain had stopped, fortunately, but there was still a bite in the air that had me wishing I'd grabbed a bigger jacket before leaving the house. The forecast of snow in a few weeks might show up sooner than we'd all expected.

I walked down the steps leading from Kathleen's house and thought back over my conversation with Paula. She'd seemed like a nice enough woman who was truly saddened at the loss of her employer. I didn't know if Paula had other clients in Pine Brook, but I wondered if there was a way to verify how she was with her other clients. Was this kind nurse look all an act for me, or was she genuinely upset about what had happened? She'd given me no evidence to the contrary, but I wasn't ready to cross anyone off my suspect list. Of course, I wasn't even certain if I had enough evidence that Kathleen had been murdered, and not simply slipped. It would probably be best if I kept all these thoughts about suspects to myself.

I had added Rebecca to the top of my list, based on what Paula had to say about her. I wasn't a stranger to tense mother-daughter relationships, but I had to wonder if things had taken a turn between the two women, particularly if Rebecca was considering putting Kathleen in a nursing home. Was Rebecca only interested in getting Kathleen's house for herself and her husband? Kathleen lived in a nice neighborhood, in a large home, and it would probably sell for a lot of money. Was that what Rebecca was after?

I came to the end of Kathleen's property and stood at the edge of her garden, looking left and right. The houses on either side of hers were built without much space between them. Though it was currently chilly and no one was strolling around outside, this seemed like the kind of neighborhood where neighbors would be chatty and friendly with each other. Might any of her neighbors know anything about what had happened to her?

I went over to the neighbor to the right. I didn't know if anyone would have more information to share about Kathleen and what had happened to her, but I figured I may as well ask.

On the house to the right of Kathleen's, a giant wreath with red and white flashing lights hung from the door, and snowman and snowflake decals were stuck to the windows all around the house. A woman answered my knock and introduced herself as Cassie. She was in her thirties, with curly blonde hair pulled back into a ponytail and a baby propped up on her hip. The baby looked out at me with wide, blue eyes.

"Such a tragedy. She was a really sweet woman," she said

after I explained why I was here. "I heard the sirens when the ambulance showed up. It was in the morning, but this little one was still sleeping. I was annoyed when the sirens woke her up, but once I realized they were going to Kathleen's house, I hurried right over to see what was going on."

"Did you notice anything strange the night before? Did you hear anything coming from Kathleen's house? Maybe see anyone standing around outside?" Detective Patel had told me that Kathleen's time of death was between ten P.M. and midnight the night before, even though Paula didn't discover her until the following morning. Which meant her killer would've been around the previous night.

She shook her head sadly. "No, sorry. I get so caught up with this one, trying to keep her busy while I work on my business. I barely pay attention to what day it is!"

Just over her shoulder, I could see piles of boxes stacked on top of each other in the hallway, spilling out into what looked like a living room further back. "What's your business?" I asked, since it seemed like the polite thing to do.

Apparently, that was the right thing to do, as her face lit up and she pulled something off the shelf next to her. "Onesies! I crochet them and sell them on Etsy. My shop is called Onesies & Twosies. Do you have any kids? I'm happy to part with one—it's practically free business." She held up the onesie in one hand. It was nicely crocheted, with the phrase *I get it from my momma* etched across the front.

I smiled and slid my hands into my pockets, afraid she might try to shove the thing at me. Cutesy baby clothes weren't really my thing. "Sorry, no kids. But they are cute. If I meet any babies, I'll be sure to send them your way."

She draped the onesie over her shoulder, using both hands to jiggle the baby, who'd begun to cry after sitting still for so long. "Thanks, I appreciate that. I better get back inside, or else this one will start screaming her head off."

I didn't want to stand in an open doorway while a baby screamed at me, so I said my goodbyes and walked back down her porch steps. No help with this neighbor. Given how busy she seemed inside, it wasn't surprising that she wouldn't notice anything going on at Kathleen's. She had heard the sirens that morning, though. Had there been a fight at Kathleen's the previous night, would she have heard that, too? While the houses were built close together, not much sound escaped from inside the houses. Unless the fight had happened on Kathleen's front yard, her entrepreneurial neighbor likely wouldn't have heard much.

I crossed in front of Kathleen's house and went over to her neighbor on the left. I didn't have high hopes for what I'd get out of this neighbor—likely just another person who thought Kathleen was great and was saddened to learn about her death—but I figured I should at least try since I was here and the rain had stopped for the moment. Of course, as I stood on the neighbor's porch and knocked on the door, a raindrop splattered against my jacket. Oh, goody.

This neighbor didn't have any Christmas decorations up, in stark contrast to Kathleen's and Cassie's houses, and all the windows had their blinds pulled shut. Was he even home?

"What?" The door was nearly ripped off its hinges in the neighbor's effort to get it open, and I took an involuntary step backwards, grasping my hands out to the side to keep myself from falling off his small porch.

Kathleen's other neighbor was older than Cassie, probably in his sixties, with a bald head and a white t-shirt that looked like it hadn't been washed in a few days. He towered over me by a few inches, and I plastered a smile on my face, hoping he wouldn't reach out and push me off his steps.

"Hi there. My name is Simone. I just came over from Kathleen's house, next door? Really tragic, what happened to her."

"Uh-huh," he grunted, crossing his arms over his chest. "What's that gotta do with me?"

"Well, I know your houses are close together. I wondered if maybe you heard anything the day she died?"

"Like what?" He narrowed his eyes at me.

I shrugged, going for a look of innocence. "I'm not so sure, that's why I'm asking. Any strange sounds coming from her house, like yelling or fighting?"

"There're all kinds of strange things happening at that house." He waved his hand flippantly towards Kathleen's home. "I see everything, and I don't like it one bit."

"What do you mean? What kinds of strange things?"

He sneered down at me. "Why's it any of your business?"

"Kathleen was a friend. I just want to make sure there wasn't anything weird going on with her death."

"Like I said, weird things were always happening at that house. Lots of singing, people wandering in and out. Very strange. But I don't know nothing about her death, except the fact that now that she's gone, maybe her roses will stop encroaching on my yard. My back garden can finally flourish once her roses die. If that's everything, I have things to get back to." Before I had a chance to respond, he slammed the door in my face, leaving me standing alone on his porch, with rain steadily dripping onto my shoulders from the overhang.

Sheesh, what was that all about? Lots of singing and people wandering in and out? And why did it seem like he was happy that Kathleen was dead?

10

I dashed off his porch, not wanting to stick around for too long. As I scurried down the path to the street, a rustling at Kathleen's house caught my attention. One of the curtains fluttered in the front window, then stilled. Was someone watching me? Paula had said she still needed to dust the curtains, so that's probably what I'd seen. I shouldn't assume everything was a sign of something nefarious going on!

I crossed the street to my car, climbing in quickly and turning on the engine so I could get the heater running. The rain had picked up and was now lashing across my windshield in heavy sheets. This was going to be fun to drive in. I rubbed my hands together as I waited for the heat to kick in, thinking back over my conversations with Kathleen's neighbors.

Cassie had seemed nice enough, though maybe a tad busy with a young child and a business. I had no idea how popular crocheted onesies were or how much money they could make you, but I wished her all the luck. Running your own business was tough work, as I knew very well.

She'd seemed genuine when she was telling me about what she'd heard the day Kathleen had died, and I could imagine she'd be so busy in her house that she wouldn't notice anything strange going on until the sirens had blared through the neighborhood. Likely, she didn't know much about Kathleen, but maybe I'd come back and visit her after a couple days, to see if anything new had come to her.

The neighbor on the other side had definitely set something off in my head. It was clear he didn't like Kathleen and didn't like getting interrupted while he was watching TV. But what had he meant about strange things going on at her house? Paula hadn't mentioned any strange goings-on, and it seemed like she'd spent a lot of time at Kathleen's house. Had Paula lied to me about what was going on at Kathleen's house, or did her neighbor just want to stir up trouble for Kathleen? And what was that thing about her roses? What did he have against roses?

I pulled away from the curb once my hands were sufficiently warmed up and headed towards my apartment to pick up Lola, before going to work at the inn. I'd ended up with more questions than answers after this excursion, and I was no closer to figuring out who might've wanted to kill Kathleen. I wasn't even all that certain that Kathleen *had* been killed, but if Detective Patel was running extra tests on her body, then she must have suspected something foul going on. Would she be willing to talk to me more about the case and the results of the tests? Only if I could bring her more proof about who killed Kathleen, and all I had right now were a bunch of rumors and odd reactions to my questions.

Rebecca and her husband David were still at the top of my suspects list. They had the clearest motive since they'd likely now inherit Kathleen's house. If Rebecca tried to move her mother into a nursing home in order to get at the house, and Kathleen didn't want to go, would Rebecca, or her bully husband, resort to using force to get what they wanted?

According to Estelle, Louise was good friends with Kathleen, but her abrupt departure at her funeral had been strange. Did Louise know something about what had happened to Kathleen that might shed light on the truth? Why had she run off so quickly like that? Would she even talk to me if I tracked her down and demanded answers? Or was she too scared about what had happened to say much more?

Was it possible *Louise* was somehow involved in all of this? She'd seemed like a kind, gentle woman, but I'd seen before that killers weren't always who you expected them to be.

Paula was another kind person in Kathleen's life who could've had something to do with her death, though I had no idea what her motive would be. As she'd told me, now that Kathleen was dead, she was out of a job. She'd been paid through the end of the month, but she was probably scrambling to find another job for herself. Unless she and Kathleen had gotten into some kind of argument, and she'd accidentally pushed the other woman down the stairs, I couldn't see a reason why Paula would want to kill Kathleen.

Of course, was she as thoughtful of a nurse as she seemed? I moved to the side of the road and pulled out my phone. Maybe The Hawthorne Nursing Group could tell me more about her.

"Hawthorne Nursing Group, how may I help you?" The woman who picked up my call sounded like she wanted to be anywhere but talking to me on the phone right now.

I went for a cheery tone in my response, to balance out her bored tone. "Hi there, I was hoping you could tell me about one of your nurses. I'm looking for assistance for my, um, mother, and a friend of mine recommended Paula. I thought I'd call to learn more about her."

Henrietta would be pretty dismayed to learn I was telling people she needed an in-home nurse, since she was barely sixty and still very active, but she didn't need to know what I was doing for the sake of this investigation.

"Oh, Paula? She's absolutely delightful! You can't go wrong with her. Always so thoughtful about her patients, going the extra mile to make sure they're taken care of. I'd be happy to set up a consultation for you with her, if you'd like to learn more."

Seemed like talking about Paula was the one thing that could add some cheeriness to this woman's voice. At least she hadn't said she was abusive or a killer. "Thanks, that's good to know. I'm considering a few different options right now, but I'll call back once I'm ready for a consultation. Have a great day!" I hung up before she could say anything else, pulling back out into traffic and continuing to my apartment.

Now I knew the Hawthorne Nursing Group liked Paula. That didn't mean she wasn't a murderer, but I was feeling less and less strongly that she had anything to do with Kathleen's death.

Lola wasn't eager about being woken up from her nap and dragged outside, but I didn't want to keep her cooped up at my apartment all day. She always liked visits to the inn, and other people could keep her busy while I worked.

As Lola settled in for a nap on the backseat, rain began falling in downtown Pine Brook. I switched on the wipers, letting the *swoosh* of the blades lull me into some semblance of peace as I drove.

It was certainly difficult looking for a killer when the

police weren't even positive that there had been a murder. Was I wasting my time, driving around in the rain and cold, questioning all these people grieving the loss of a great woman? Was Estelle making a bigger deal out of nothing? Estelle was determined, though, particularly once she got a bee in her bonnet about something, and I didn't think she'd listen to me unless I could find definitive proof that Kathleen hadn't been killed. Of course, how do you go about finding evidence that something *didn't* happen?

Rain was now pouring down in buckets as I parked at the inn, and I tossed my raincoat over my head and dashed inside the building with Lola at my side, shivering from the cold. While I enjoyed the Christmas holidays as much as anyone else, I was looking forward to spring.

In the lobby, Tracy and Nick stood at the front desk, and my shoulders relaxed as I spotted them. These two could help distract me from this murder investigation, or convince me that I was making a mistake and needed to keep my nose out of things.

"Hey, what's going on?" I said as I approached the front desk, leaning in to give Nick a kiss on the lips. Before I had a chance to reach him, though, he straightened up, his eyes wide, and mumbled something about needing to go, then dashed out of the inn.

I turned to Tracy, frowning at this sudden departure. "What's going on with him?"

Tracy smirked and dropped her gaze to the ledger in front of her. "Nothing. He said he had some work to get back to, so he couldn't stay and chat."

I glanced back over my shoulder, pursing my lips as I processed this excuse. "He had to leave so quickly, he couldn't even give his girlfriend a kiss?"

Tracy waved her hand nonchalantly. "He's just busy. Nothing to worry about."

"Okay," I said slowly, turning back to the front desk. "And what exactly were you two chatting about?"

Her eyes widened briefly, surprise flashing across her face, then she quickly rearranged her features into a neutral expression. "Our next shipment of produce, of course. What else would Nick and I have to talk about?"

Why was she acting so weird right now? And why had he really run off like that? I trusted both of them, so I didn't think there was anything weird going on between them, but they were acting strange.

"Estelle mentioned you're looking into Kathleen's death," Tracy went on, smoothly transitioning the conversation away to another topic and ruffling Lola's ears as the dog settled onto her bed behind the front desk. "What have you learned so far?"

I sighed, still confused as to why Tracy and Nick were acting so weird, but also needing to talk through the case with someone. I could question Nick later when I went home that night.

"Not much," I said, moving to stand behind the front desk. "Her daughter has the clearest motive since she'll now inherit Kathleen's house, and she'd been trying to get her mother to move into a nursing home, but Kathleen didn't want to go. If she needed the money, she might've decided it was easier to get rid of her mom instead of convincing her to move."

"Wow, that's pretty brutal. And over a house? I mean, I know people have killed for a lot of strange things in this town, but she must've really hated her mom."

"Or really needed the house. I agree it's a strong reaction to something like that, and I'm not even really sure if that's what happened. The police are still saying officially that Kathleen's death was an accident, so I can't even be certain there's a killer out there."

"If the police say it was an accident, then why are you looking into it?"

"Estelle. She's convinced Kathleen never would have fallen like that, that someone must've pushed her. She found her house in shambles and thinks someone was looking for something, but I found everything cleaned up when I visited her house earlier today. Plus, one of her friends said that Kathleen had been unsteady on her feet recently."

"Sounds like it was probably an accident, then. Why keep investigating?"

"I'm not sure if the police really believe it was an accident. I heard from Miriam that Detective Patel had ordered extra tests on Kathleen's body, but she didn't know what the tests were or what the results were. If Patel is having tests run, maybe she thinks there's more going on here, but doesn't want the killer to get spooked and leave town by calling it murder."

"Hmm, maybe." Tracy leaned back against the counter, gazing off to the side thoughtfully. "It seems like you might be getting yourself involved in something that may not even be murder. I mean, I suppose if there's no killer, then you're not at risk by asking all these questions, but I can't imagine people are happy with what you're insinuating. Are you sure you want to do this?"

"I've been having those same thoughts, honestly. But it does seem like there's more going on here than meets the eye. Estelle is determined to find Kathleen's killer, so rather than let her run around, potentially getting hurt, I figured I could ask some questions and see what I can find out."

"Well, I think you should stay out of things, but as long as you're not getting hurt, then I guess I can't make you stop." She flipped through a few envelopes on the front desk, pulling out a large one. "Oh, look, Dr. Li sent us a Christmas card. That's kind of her."

She held out the thick card-stock, and I studied the smiling snowman and *Happy Holidays!* on the card. Deborah Li was a doctor in town who I'd once accused of murder. Apparently, she wasn't upset about that anymore if she was sending us Christmas cards. I added *Send Christmas cards* to my mental list of tasks I still needed to complete this month, along with *Buy Christmas tree* and *Find out why boyfriend has been acting so weird*. It was going to be a busy month!

Penny came out of the bistro just then, wringing her hands together. "One of the guests said their toilet is overflowing," she said once she was at the front desk. "They're worried it might be leaking through the floor to the room down below. Can one of you help out?"

Tracy sighed and shut the ledger closed. "I'll handle this. You stay here. I think some guests are coming down soon to check out." She followed after Penny and headed upstairs to find the offending toilet.

Before I knew it, I had a line of guests almost out the door—okay, maybe that was a slight exaggeration, but there was suddenly a large group of people needing help from me. Checking in, checking out, asking for directions to the spa or the bistro. Sometimes the inn got like this, where we'd have waves of busyness in an otherwise quiet day. I worked my way through the line as quickly as I could, keeping an eye on the stairs in case Tracy came back down. The line just seemed to get longer and longer, until, finally, the last guest left, content with directions to the spa and a brochure of all of our services, and I slumped against the front desk, exhausted. Hunting for a potential killer and running an inn was getting pretty tiring!

Tracy strolled down the stairs a few moments later, sauntering over to the front desk. "All good upstairs. That's the third clog this month. We may want to consider updating all the toilets. Everything okay?" she asked, noticing the exhaustion on my face.

"Yeah," I said, rubbing a hand across my face. "Just tired. Things got really busy once you left. I wish Nadia were here to help out."

"Don't worry, she'll be back soon." Tracy went back to flipping through the ledger, making notes as she read the pages.

I let out a sigh. Nadia would be back soon, but then Tracy would be gone for six months, and I'd be stuck dealing with all this chaos again. Could the inn handle Tracy being gone for so long on her vacation with Isabella? Could I?

"Simone, there you are!" My mom came striding down the stairs, waving at me as she crossed the lobby.

Tracy straightened up beside me, then darted out from behind the front desk and raced down the hallway towards my office, mumbling something about needing to do some paperwork. I smirked as she left. Clearly, she still hadn't worked up the courage to talk to my mom about her relationship with Sylvia and was now avoiding her completely.

"Where's Tracy off to?" my mom asked once she was at the front desk.

"She's got some paperwork to take care of. I'm sorry I haven't been around much today. Have you been having a nice time?"

"Yes, absolutely! Your spa is wonderful. I've already had a facial and a massage today, and I'm scheduled to get waxed this afternoon. I'm going to be a new woman once I return home to your father!"

I smiled and murmured my agreement, trying not to think about what my mom was going to get waxed later that day. "I'm glad you're having fun. What else do you have planned for today?"

"Let's go Christmas shopping! You said you needed to get something for Nick, right? You can show me around town, too."

I hesitated for a moment. I was still tired after the onslaught of guests we'd just had and the sleuthing I'd done this morning, and I felt bad about leaving Tracy behind to deal with any other waves of busyness. But I also felt bad because I hadn't been spending much time with my mom since she'd gotten to town. Tracy could handle things for a couple hours, couldn't she? She was always so much better at managing the inn than I was.

"Sure, let's go," I said, shooting off a text to Tracy and letting her know where I was going to be.

My mom and I headed downtown in my car. Fortunately, the rain had stopped, though there was still a sharp chill in the air. Pine Brook had set up a giant holiday market in a set of town-owned buildings near downtown, normally reserved for town meetings and other tourist attractions, and that's where we went.

Strings of lights were looped around the streetlights in town, blinking on and off in the gloomy day. The holiday market was a buzz of activity when we arrived, and we strolled down the aisles, looking around at different trinkets.

"Ooh, what about this?" my mom asked, pointing to a popcorn maker. "Men love popcorn, don't they?"

I chuckled. "Sometimes. But I don't think that's quite right for Nick."

We continued on, stopping at a booth full of bath soaps and lotions, testing out different samples. The woman who owned the booth smiled as she watched us smell the different scents.

"I make these all myself," she explained, pointing to a sign where she'd listed out the instructions for making homemade soap. "I think the soap works better when you make it yourself."

"What a lovely idea," Mom said. "I'll take these." She held up two bars, and the woman behind the booth packed them up for her, ringing up her order.

"That was fast. I thought we were here for my shopping?" I asked jokingly.

"I can't stop myself when I'm around homemade soap. I've had to stop going to the farmer's market near our house because I kept coming back with soap I'd never use."

I chuckled as we continued strolling down the aisles, looking at the different products for sale. I'd considered bringing up Sylvia's letter again, now that I had her alone, but I didn't want to ruin the mood. My mom obviously didn't want to talk about it, likely because it was a difficult topic for her, and I didn't want to push her when we were trying to have a happy shopping trip together. I'd been so busy at the inn, we'd barely spent any time together, and I wanted this trip to go well.

"Oh, look at these gingerbread houses!" Mom dashed over to another booth, peering down at the intricately made houses. "Remember when we tried to make gingerbread houses that one year?"

"Yes, and I remember getting into a fight with Chrissy because she thought I stole some of her gumdrops for my house. How you put up with the two of us when we were kids, I'll never know." I chuckled.

She smiled and looped her arm through mine, leading us away from the gingerbread houses. "You two were darlings. Feisty, but I wouldn't trade your childhood for anything. I'm glad we get to spend this time together."

"Me too. Ooh, hot chocolate!" I led her over to another booth selling cups of creamy cocoa, buying us each a cup.

"Now, dear, I don't mean to pry," she said once we walked away from the hot chocolate stand, cradling our cups.

I groaned. "Not a great way to start a sentence."

She smirked. "Well, we are here to find Nick a present, right? Tell me what's going on with him. You two seem great together. Where do you see things going with him?"

I sighed, picking at the lid of my cup. "I don't know… I mean, I love him, I really do. I guess I'm just scared, you know? I want our relationship to develop, but it's scary to make that next move."

"I understand." She took a sip of her hot chocolate. "You know your father and I met when we were in med school, right? That's one of the most stressful times of any person's life. I saw so many relationships not make it through the chaos of med school or becoming a doctor. But with your father…well, sometimes, when you know, you just know. And I knew with him. I didn't want anyone else."

I smiled at her words. She was right. Relationships always had their hard parts, but the truly great relationships made those hard parts worth it. With Nick, I knew that we were meant to be together, just like my mom did with my dad. I needed to get over my fear and let him know that I wanted to take our relationship to the next level.

"What about this?" My mom's voice interrupted my ruminations, and I found her standing at another booth featuring leather wallets that you could get engraved with initials. "Men always love their wallets."

"That's not a bad idea," I said, running my hand across the smooth leather. "He was just telling me how cumbersome his current wallet has been. How long does the engraving take?" I asked the man behind the booth.

"Just a couple days, and we'll deliver it straight to you once it's done," he said with a smile.

"Great. I'll take this one," I said, pointing to a light brown, buttery, smooth wallet that I knew Nick would love. I jotted down the engraving details on an order form, then passed it back to the owner of the booth, along with my credit card.

"Happy holidays!" he called out once he'd finished my order and passed me a receipt. I tucked it into my pocket and hurried after my mom, pleased that I'd found something thoughtful for Nick.

My mom was standing a few feet away, at the intersection of three different aisles, staring at something in the corner as other customers milled around her. "Oh, dear," she said once I was at her side, pointing towards a couple standing in a corner, away from any of the booths.

I followed her finger, spotting Rebecca and David in the corner. David was looming over Rebecca, his face red, but they were too far away for us to hear what they were saying. Based on the look on her face, it didn't seem good. She flinched as he raised his hand, and a shiver ran through me.

I took a step closer, feeling compelled to interrupt whatever was happening here, when a surge of customers passed in front of me, jostling me where I stood and knocking me backwards a couple steps. My mom rushed over and grabbed me before I had a chance to stumble.

"Are you okay?" she asked once the crowd had passed and I was steady again.

"Yes, I—"I started, then stopped once I looked back up and saw that David and Rebecca had disappeared from their corner. My head whipped around, looking for the couple, but there were too many people around to see much of anything.

"Did you know them?" she asked.

I nodded. "That was Kathleen's daughter and son-in-law. It looked...well, it looked like he might've been about to hurt her. But I can't be sure..." My voice trailed off as I strained to find them and make sense of what I'd just seen.

"Oh, my. Should we call the police?"

They were nowhere in sight, and I wasn't even really sure what I had seen. I shook my head, defeated. "No, but I think it's probably best if we get back to the inn. I'm all out of the holiday spirit now."

"Of course. At least you got something for Nick, and I have some new soap to try out." She looped her arm back through mine and led me out of the market, while thoughts of Rebecca and David and what I'd seen between them ran through my head.

11

Back at the inn, the lobby was quiet, a fire crackling in the fireplace. My stomach grumbled as we hung up our coats.

"I think things should be quiet for a little while," I said. "Why don't we grab lunch?"

"Sounds great!" My mom's smile was cheery. The woman sure did love her food.

We strolled into the bistro, which wasn't super busy on this weekday, and I motioned to Eddy that we were going to grab a table in the corner. He came over with menus and got our drink orders, then my mom and I settled into our seats.

"Tell me all about this murder investigation," my mom said, launching right into things. At least she wasn't going to tell me about her wax later today.

"There's not much to tell," I said, fiddling with my menu as I pondered what to order. "I went by Kathleen's house earlier today to meet her nurse. She'd cleaned up everything, so I didn't see that mess you and Estelle had found earlier this week."

"What did you think about her nurse?"

"Paula seemed nice enough. I don't know what reason she'd have to kill Kathleen. Now that Kathleen's dead, she's out of a job."

"Why is she still at her house? You'd think she'd leave and go find another job, right?"

"She's paid through the end of the month, and she said she wanted to help Rebecca take care of things at her mom's house. Packing up boxes and all of that. It seemed pretty considerate of her, actually."

"Yes, I suppose so. Although she is getting paid, right? So she's not being completely selfless. What do you think about Kathleen's daughter?"

"She seems to have the strongest motive since she'll now inherit Kathleen's house. Apparently, she'd been trying to move her mom into a nursing home, but Kathleen wouldn't go. If she wanted her house to sell it, which her husband said is what they were going to do now, then maybe she didn't want to wait for it to happen."

"But if they sold Kathleen's house, wouldn't the money still go to Kathleen? Or to paying the nursing home bills?"

I considered that for a moment. "You might be right. But her husband was very interested in selling the house now. Maybe they thought there was some way they could get the proceeds from the sale with Kathleen in the nursing home. Now that she's gone, there's nothing standing in their way of getting the money."

Mom shivered. "I can't imagine killing your own mother for a house. Seems so heartless."

"I agree, but people have killed for less, I suppose. I also talked to Kathleen's neighbors while I was there earlier. One of them was really busy with a baby and a business and didn't hear anything, but the other neighbor was a real grump. In fact, he was happy that Kathleen was dead since now her roses wouldn't encroach on her garden. I wouldn't be surprised if he got upset with her about her roses and pushed her in anger."

Eddy approached our table and set down our drinks. "Are you talking about Joseph? He's definitely a grump. He and Kathleen were always getting into fights."

"Really?" I straightened up in my seat, becoming alert. "Often?"

Eddy nodded. "In fact, they got into a big argument a few days ago. Something about her roses getting in the way of his lavender plant? I don't know exactly what it was about, but he definitely threatened to hurt her if she didn't deal with her flowers. It was loud enough, you could hear it from three blocks away!"

I didn't think it likely that their fight could be heard from so far away—Eddy was known for his exaggerations—but I wasn't surprised that news of this big fight had made its rounds in the town gossip mill. It was interesting that this was the first time I was hearing about it. Did Estelle know about the fight?

It made sense that Joseph the neighbor wouldn't have said anything about it when I went to question him, but now I had some questions about whether anything else had happened after that argument between the two of them, maybe behind closed doors.

"Thanks, Eddy. Mom, I'm sorry about this, but I have to go. I need to tell the police about this fight." I made to stand up, but my mom reached out and grabbed my wrist before I could leave.

"Wait, you can't go to the police with a rumor. We need actual evidence for them! Let's go talk to that neighbor again. If we tell him what we know, maybe we'll catch him in a lie, and he'll spill the beans."

"I don't know," I said slowly, sitting back down. "Seems like a bad idea to confront a suspected killer with no real proof, just a rumor."

"Don't worry, we'll be fine. There'll be two of us, and I'll make sure to have nine-one-one ready to go on my phone, in case things go bad. Come on, let's go get this guy!" She hopped up from her seat and dashed out of the bistro, leaving me to stare after her.

Now I was going to go question a suspect with my mother in tow? This whole investigation was turning into one big, bad mistake. But I had no choice now because I didn't want her going after Joseph alone. I motioned to Eddy that we were leaving, then hurried after my mom.

Outside, the temperature had dropped several degrees. Looked like that forecasted snow might be here before we knew it. I glanced up at the darkening sky, wishing I was inside the inn with a mug of hot tea and a book, rather than running around town with my mother, searching for a killer who may or may not exist. Maybe Kathleen's neighbor Joseph wouldn't even be home, and we'd have to leave without talking to him.

As I drove us across town, my mom chattered from the passenger seat about her spa treatments that morning and whether she'd have to reschedule her waxing now that we were off investigating a murder. I kept my gaze steady on the road in front of me, my hands tight on the steering wheel. We were alone and in private, so now might've been the best time to bring up Sylvia's letter again, but I couldn't get myself to do it. I didn't want to set my mom off again, and I worried that she'd be even more resistant to talking to me about what had happened between her and Sylvia. Maybe I should just wait until she was ready to talk to me? That could be years from now, though.

I came to a stop in front of Joseph's house, and we climbed out of my car. Kathleen's house was dark and silent next door. Paula must've gone home for the day. A couple lights were on in Joseph's house, though we couldn't see any movement from outside. We hurried up to his front door and I knocked, part of me hoping he wouldn't be home so that we could leave and take all this to the police. Again, I noticed the lack of Christmas decorations outside his home. He still hadn't gotten into the holiday spirit? Maybe he had more decorations inside.

No answer to my initial knock, so I knocked again, trying to keep a smile from crossing my face at the realization that I wouldn't have to confront Joseph today. My mom furrowed her brow and poked her head into a window next to the front door, but the blinds were closed and she couldn't see anything. She walked down the porch, sticking her head around the side of the house.

"Mom, we should go. He's obviously not here, or doesn't want to talk to us."

"We came all the way down here, we shouldn't leave so fast. That's probably his car, right?" She pointed to a Toyota in the driveway. "And a bunch of lights are on. If you're going to prove to the police that Kathleen was killed, then we need to talk to this guy about his fight with her."

I glanced at the time on my watch. "It's getting late. I should get back to the inn. And don't you have a wax appointment to get to?" As much as I wanted to forget about that appointment, maybe it would convince her.

She brushed away my concerns like a fly. "That can all wait. We need to get answers." She went to the other end of the porch and poked her head around the side of the house. "You said he was a gardener, right? I'm assuming it's in the back since I don't see any flowers up here."

She was right—Joseph's front yard was only grass, and not the plants that would get encroached on by Kathleen's roses. Plus, I didn't see Kathleen's roses in her front yard, either. Their gardens must've been in the back.

"I think you're right," I said, going to stand next to my mom. "But what does that have to do with anything?"

"Maybe he's in his garden, and that's why he's not answering the door. We should go back there and check on him." She turned to step off the porch and walk around the back of his house, but I grabbed her arm before she could go.

"Wait, we can't just go around sticking our noses into people's yards. I think this might be trespassing! Besides, who gardens when it's this cold outside?"

"True gardeners, that's who. Don't worry, we'll be fine!" Before I could stop her, she hopped off the porch and scurried down the side of Joseph's house.

I sighed, debating the merits of leaving her and heading straight home to burrow under my covers with a book, but I knew I couldn't do that. Instead, I took another deep breath for courage, then hurried after her.

The path on the side of Joseph's house led straight back to his garden, which was gorgeous, even in the winter. Few plants were blooming, but the vibrant greens hinted at the beautiful flowers that would blossom in the spring. His yard extended several feet back, ending at a fence so far back, it doubled the size of his property. Kathleen's yard was much smaller on the other side of the property line, but I could see where her roses were already beginning to encroach on his side. I wondered if Rebecca and David knew who they were going to have to deal with now that those roses belonged to them.

"That's strange." My mom stood in the middle of Joseph's yard, staring at his house.

"What?" I asked, turning my attention away from where Kathleen's roses had begun to tangle around Joseph's plants.

"The back door is open. Why would he leave the door open in this cold?"

I went to stand next to my mom, both of us peering through the open back door. The yard led into his kitchen, but there were fewer lights on back here, and we couldn't see much further into his house.

Suddenly, my mom grabbed my arm, squeezing tight. "What if he's hurt in there? Maybe he fell and hit his head? We should check on him."

"We can't just walk into his house, even if the door is open. That's definitely a crime. Give me a minute to get a little closer." I approached the back door, taking slow steps so as not to scare him if he was on the other side of the door. "Joseph?" I called out as I got closer, but there was no answer.

As I stood on the threshold of his back door, peering into his kitchen, I quickly realized why we hadn't gotten a response. Joseph was sprawled out on the floor of his kitchen, a coffee mug lying beside him. Based on the stillness of his body, and the way his tongue lolled out the side of his bloated face, I didn't need to get too close to know he was very dead.

12

The police arrived quickly after our call to emergency services. I'd taken a couple steps into Joseph's house to check his pulse, but his bulging neck and discolored face clearly indicated that he wasn't getting up any time soon. My mom and I stood just outside his house as we waited for the police to arrive, holding each other close to keep the chill away.

Officer Scott, one of the more experienced cops at the Pine Brook Police Department (even though he looked seventeen), was the first officer on the scene, and he didn't seem too surprised to see me.

"Where's the body?" he asked.

"In the kitchen," I said, pointing over my shoulder, my teeth chattering from the cold.

He strode past us into the house, then came back out several minutes later. "The rest of the house is empty. Did you touch anything in the kitchen?"

We shook our heads no in unison.

"All right." Officer Scott nodded, then spoke a few words into his walkie-talkie. "Let's go wait inside his living room so you don't freeze out here. I've got a few questions for you both."

We followed him inside the house, averting our gazes from the kitchen. We settled onto a couch in the living room, which was sparsely furnished and quiet. No decorations inside, either. How sad was that? The most vibrant part of his home was outside. Seemed like Joseph spent most of his time in his garden. Or at least, he used to. Now, he wouldn't spend any more time in that garden.

"Tell me what happened," Officer Scott said once we were seated and had stopped shivering.

I quickly took him through what had happened, how we'd knocked on Joseph's front door but hadn't gotten a response, then decided to go around back to see if he was in the garden, and had instead found his back door open, letting in the cold.

As I spoke, more police officers filed into the kitchen from the back door, a few spreading out to search for evidence in the rest of his house. My mom gripped my hand tightly, her lips pressed together in a thin line as I spoke.

"And why were you here in the first place? Did you know the victim?" Scott asked.

I hesitated, then shook my head. "Not well. He was neighbors with Kathleen. I came by earlier this morning to ask him if he'd seen anything suspicious at her house before her death. Then, I learned about a fight the two of them had before she died, so I came back to ask him about that." I didn't want to lie to the police about what I'd really been doing here, but the truth sounded pretty bad to me.

Scott stilled at my words. "And why exactly were you asking questions about a death that's been ruled an accident?"

"I've just had some questions about what really

happened. And now her neighbor is dead—that does look pretty suspicious."

Scott sighed, then stood up. "Stay here. I need to check on something." He left us sitting alone, going into the kitchen to talk to the other police officers.

"Kathleen must've been murdered," my mom whispered from my side. "Why else would Joseph be killed, too?"

"We don't know that he was murdered. Maybe it was also an accident." His discolored and distorted face didn't look like an accident, though.

Two cops left the kitchen and strode through the living room to the front door, talking to each other. "Peanut allergy," one said to the other, not seeming to realize we were sitting in the living room. "I found an EpiPen in his pocket with a label indicating a severe peanut allergy. Looks like the poor guy didn't get to it fast enough."

Once we were alone again, I leaned over to my mom. "See? It was an accident. He must've ingested peanuts without realizing it."

"Hmm. I don't know. Seems suspicious that this would happen so soon after Kathleen's death. Maybe there's more going on here."

Before I had a chance to respond, Officer Scott came back into the living room. "You two are free to leave, but please make yourselves available for additional questions. I'm sure Detective Patel will have a lot of questions for you about why you were here in the first place," he added to me, his gaze stern.

"I'll make sure to pick up when she calls." I grabbed my mom's arm and yanked her out of Joseph's house, out into the cold of the December afternoon.

All my mom could talk about on the drive back to the inn was Joseph's death and how likely it was that both he and Kathleen had been murdered. I wasn't so sure if I believed it, though. Maybe he hadn't realized he was eating peanuts, and hadn't gotten to his EpiPen in time. Still, if he had one of those in his pocket, you'd think he would have noticed the signs of an allergic reaction quickly and been able to save himself. Had something more nefarious happened?

Estelle was waiting for us back at the inn when we returned. "There you are," she said, hurrying over to our sides and dragging us into a corner of the lobby as soon as we walked in. "Eddy said you'd gone to talk to Kathleen's neighbor, Joseph. What happened?"

I glanced around the lobby, but we seemed to be alone. I didn't think the police would want me blabbing this information around town, but there was clearly more going on than we'd originally thought, and Estelle deserved to know what was happening.

"We found him dead in his kitchen," I said, keeping my voice low. "Looks like an allergic reaction. The police think he ingested peanuts and didn't get to his EpiPen in time. Seems like an accident."

"Hmm," Estelle said thoughtfully. "I'm not so sure about that. I remember Kathleen telling me about his allergy. Apparently, it was pretty bad. She tried to bring him cookies once, a few years ago, as a peace offering to stop all of their fighting, but he'd gotten upset with her. She knew about his allergy, so she'd made sure to make sugar cookies, but she couldn't say for certain whether or not any of the ingredients she'd used had that 'may contain nuts' warning. He was worried about cross-contamination."

"I told you it wasn't an accident," my mom said excitedly. "No way would someone with that bad of an allergy accidentally eat peanuts. Someone must've given them to him."

Peanut allergies could be pretty severe, and if Joseph wasn't even willing to eat cookies without knowing if the ingredients had that warning, then it didn't seem likely that he'd allow anything that had been near peanuts into his house.

"I need to talk to Detective Patel about this and make sure she knows about his severe allergy," I said. "She'll probably be too busy with his death today, but I'll go see her first thing in the morning. You two need to keep quiet about this, okay? If there is a killer out there, they can't know what we know."

They both agreed to keep their mouths shut, then hurried off to the bistro, discussing new motives. I sighed and rubbed my hands against my temples as they left. Looked like we were now dealing with a killer in Pine Brook, again. Who would be next?

THE NEXT DAY, I left my house early to meet Detective Patel at the police station. I'd texted her the night before, asking if we could meet to discuss Joseph's death. She must've been interested in getting my statement about what had happened, as she immediately responded and agreed to meet the next morning.

Snow had fallen overnight and a light dusting of white covered the world as I slowly made my way to the police department, the heater on full blast. I'd left Lola snuggled up warm under the covers, trying not to be jealous of a dog as I left my apartment.

I passed the Christmas tree in town square as I drove, now with snowflakes dotting the pine needles and ornaments. Once again reminding me that I still didn't have a tree or any decorations in my apartment. I had a killer to catch, though—I was a little busy!

The police station was quiet when I entered, the front desk empty. Detective Patel was seated on one of the benches near the front door, scrolling through her phone, and she jumped up when I came in.

"Tweeting?" I asked, pointing to her phone with a smirk.

She rolled her eyes but cracked a smile. "It's too early for Twitter. Come on back."

She led me through the police station, which was mostly empty this early in the morning. A couple other officers were seated at desks in the main bullpen, but this wasn't nearly as busy as I'd seen the station before. Guess sometimes Pine Brook's police officers usually got a later start to their day. Or maybe they were still at Joseph's, collecting evidence about his death.

Patel led me to one of the conference rooms, stopping off at the coffee station set up in the back. She made me a cup, adding the right amount of cream and sugar to my mug, then passed it to me. I held back a smile at the thrill of realizing that she knew how I took my coffee.

Once in the conference room, she settled onto a chair on one side of the table and pulled out a pen and notepad. "All right, what's going on? How did you end up finding another dead body yesterday?"

I took a sip of my coffee, giving myself a moment to collect myself. I'd planned what I'd wanted to say the night before, but I found that my thoughts always got scattered once I was actually sitting in the police station. Something about the threat of getting locked up that got me all out of sorts.

"I heard that Joseph, Kathleen's neighbor, had gotten into an argument with Kathleen before her death. I went to his home to ask him about it, and my mom and I found his back door open. That's when I saw his body inside, so I called the police."

"And why exactly were you going to ask him questions about Kathleen? Given that her death has been ruled an accident."

"Come on, Detective, we both know there's more going on with her death—especially now that her neighbor has turned up dead, too. I have a feeling you know there's more going on here than just another accident."

Patel sighed and rubbed her eyes. "Why do you insist on getting involved in my cases? Are you trying to make things hard for me?"

I squirmed in my seat. "It's not intentional. You just happen to be the cop in town who always ends up with these murders. And you do a good job of solving them, too, often with some help from me. I'd assume you'd be more open to what I can offer."

Patel raised one shoulder in defeat. "You do often have some good ideas. But I can't keep letting a civilian stick her nose into these cases."

I leaned forward, looking for anything that might get her to open up to me. "Joseph had a bad peanut allergy. Did you know that? Apparently, he wouldn't let anything with peanuts into his house. You really think he's going to accidentally ingest peanuts like that? He had an EpiPen on him, for Pete's sake! He was prepared for this kind of thing."

"How do you know about his allergy?" she asked accusingly.

"Everyone knew about it," I said casually. "He wouldn't even accept cookies from his neighbors if they couldn't prove that they hadn't been cross-contaminated. No way does he accidentally eat peanuts."

Patel rested her head in her hand, staring off to the side. "I shouldn't even be talking to you about any of this. As Head Detective, I'm under a lot of pressure to solve these things quickly, and I can't go around sharing information with a civilian. Especially not when our official statement says these were accidents. And I can't have you sticking your nose in where it doesn't belong, either. I could get into a lot of trouble here."

"You have to admit that I've been helpful. Who knows how long it would've taken to find Joseph's body if I hadn't gone to talk to him? If there's really a killer out there, don't you want to try to catch them?"

"Obviously I do, but that doesn't mean I can just go around telling you all these details. I'm under a lot of pressure now and I need to be much more careful about the things I tell people."

"Oh, come on, it can't be that bad. Chief Tate goes around blabbing about things like this all the time. Remember last summer, when he told a bunch of people at Cuppa Joe's that the Peeping Tom running around was one of the high school kids? He doesn't seem to follow the rules."

"Yeah, well, it's different for him. It's different for all the men in this department. I have to work twice as hard to get even half as far as them, and I have to watch everything I say. Even as Head Detective, it's still hard to gain a slice of respect in this old boys' club."

I never realized how tough Patel had it here, but it made sense. Being surrounded by cops who all thought they knew what was best, and who never wanted to listen to what she had to say, had to be hard. I was lucky to be surrounded by supportive women at the Hemlock, and I couldn't imagine how challenging it would be to do my job if I didn't have the respect of my employees.

I sat forward in my seat, gripping my cup between my hands. "Look, I promise I'll keep this all to myself. And if you really believe that Kathleen's death was an accident, then tell me that, and I'll leave. But if there's any chance there's something else going on here, maybe I can help. Estelle is certain Kathleen was killed, and now that Joseph has likely been murdered, it's looking like she's right. I don't want anyone else to get hurt, and if there's a killer out there, I need to warn Estelle to be careful about whom she talks to."

I was grasping at straws now, looking for any way to convince Patel to open up to me, but as she took a few breaths and kept her gaze down, I thought maybe my pleas might have been working.

Patel grimaced, lowering her eyes to the desk separating us. She didn't speak, and I held my breath, not wanting to do anything that might set her off or raise her guards again.

Finally, she spoke. "I can't have Estelle going around potentially putting herself in the line of fire, so I'll tell you one thing: Kathleen's death may have been a murder. We've already told Kathleen's daughter about this and plan on making a statement later this afternoon, so I'm not telling you anything you wouldn't have found out shortly. We ran some extra tests on the bruising on her body, and based on the position of the bruises, it's looking like she was pushed."

"Pushed?"

"Pushed."

So Miriam was right—Patel had run those extra tests and thought there was more going on here. "Why did you run more tests after saying it was an accident?"

"After you came to me, concerned about her death, I

talked to the medical examiner and asked her to take a closer look at the body. We'd noticed bruising on her body after the initial ME report, including bruising around her neck. We assumed the bruises came from her fall, but I had the doctor take a closer look. Not only was Kathleen pushed, based on bruising on her back, but it looks like someone might've tried to strangle her first, too, based on marks on her neck. Something must've gone wrong with the strangulation, because then she was pushed."

I sat back in my seat, stunned. "Wow. I'm surprised you actually listened to me, especially since I didn't have very much evidence when I came to you."

Patel shrugged. "You've been right about a lot of these things in the past. We had Kathleen's body for several hours before we were required to release it to her family, so I didn't think it would hurt to let the doctor take a closer look. Once she confirmed what she found, it was easy to launch a full investigation."

"So what does this mean? Are you officially investigating Kathleen's death?"

"While the evidence Dr. Haynes found was convincing, even she admitted that it could be explained by a few different things. There's still a chance that Kathleen took a bad fall and went down harder than we originally assumed. If it was an accident, then no one was at home with her, and we really can't say with certainty how she fell. But there might be more going on here than we realized, and that's something I need to look into."

"Joseph's death must be related, right? Maybe he learned something about Kathleen's killer, so they decided to get rid of him, too."

"At this point, we're not eliminating any options until we know more about what happened to the two of them. Now, you need to stay out of this and you need to tell Estelle to do the same. We're potentially dealing with a very dangerous killer, and I can't let anyone else die."

"I'll be careful. Thank you for sharing all of this with me."

My mind raced as Patel led me out of the station and I hurried to my car. Estelle was right—Kathleen had been killed, and her killer had gone after Joseph, as well. What did he know that would lead to his death? And had I already spoken to the killer and let them know that I was onto them?

I'd told Patel that I would stay out of things, but now that I knew Estelle was right, I had to keep digging. I didn't want her taking over the investigation, so I had to find more proof about who had killed Kathleen and bring it to the police. Soon, they were going to reveal that they were searching for a killer, and I didn't want the killer to flee town before we had a chance to stop them.

13

As I drove around town, I couldn't stop thinking about this bombshell from Detective Patel. She had strong doubts that Kathleen's death was an accident, and she was going to announce a formal investigation later today. Once Patel made things official and made her announcement about an investigation, what would the killer do next?

They'd already proven that they were willing to kill again. After Kathleen's fall, they could have gone to the police, claiming it was an accident and that she'd slipped and fallen. But now that the killer had gone after Joseph, poisoning him with his lethal allergy, things had changed.

If I went back to the inn, Estelle would show up and start pestering me for more information about the case. I didn't like lying to her, but I also didn't want her to know what I'd learned from Patel yet. She'd find out soon enough, and I wanted some time to myself to process this new information and figure out what I thought about it. Estelle would want to go back to all of the suspects and start grilling them about their whereabouts on the night Kathleen was killed. I didn't want to spook anyone before the police made their official statement, but maybe I could go back to some people I'd already talked to and ask them some questions about Joseph, now that he was dead.

Was there more evidence at Kathleen's house about her murder? I didn't think I'd be able to snoop around Joseph's house now that the police were treating it as a crime scene, but if Paula was still helping to pack up Kathleen's house, maybe she'd let me in and I could take another look around.

I parked in front of Kathleen's house and got out of my car, shivering in the cold. Most of the snow that had been on the ground had melted by this point in the morning, but heavy, gray clouds hung in the sky, portending more snow later tonight. A hot mug of tea and a cuddly blanket flashed through my mind as I shoved my hands deep into my jacket pockets and walked up the steps to Kathleen's front door. Why did I agree to investigate a murder during winter? Moving forward, I was only going to take on cases in the spring or summer time, when the weather was hot and I didn't mind running around town, grilling suspects.

"Simone. What are you doing here?" Paula looked mighty surprised to see me when she opened the front door. She had a wash cloth tossed over her shoulder, a silver serving platter in her hand.

"I'm sorry to interrupt. Do you mind if I come in for a minute?"

She hesitated for just a moment, then nodded and stepped back to let me through. "I'm sorry, of course, please come in. I didn't expect to see you out there. I'm still packing up some of Kathleen's boxes," she added, waving the silver platter in the air as she led me back to the kitchen.

"How's packing coming along?" I asked, settling onto a stool in the kitchen while Paula set the serving platter down on the counter.

"Tea?" She motioned to the kettle and I nodded. "Slowly but surely," she went on as she filled up the kettle and pulled out mugs. "You never realize how much stuff you accumulate over the years, especially once you get to Kathleen's age. I'm not sure if Rebecca realizes how much she's going to have to deal with once everything is packed up and they sell the house."

"It's kind of you to stick around and help get everything organized and in boxes. I'm sure they've got a lot going on right now."

"Like I said before, I don't mind it. I know how it is packing up your parents' belongings. I wanted to make things easier for them. Plus, I've already been paid through the end of the month, and I'm still looking for my next gig. Pine Brook doesn't have as many elderly people looking for nurses as I would've thought."

"Do you live in town?"

She shook her head. "Holliston. Have you been before?"

I nodded, gratefully accepting the mug she passed across the counter to me. I'd spent time in Holliston investigating a college professor's death the year before, when my sister had come to town. It seemed like a nice enough town, though not someplace that I was eager to return to.

"Not that I don't love the company," Paula said, leaning against the kitchen counter with her mug in hand. "But did you come by for a specific reason? It's about time I took a break, so I don't mind chatting, but I'm just surprised to see you here."

"I wanted to check on you and see how things were

going. I heard about the death next door. Given what happened to Kathleen, it seems like there might be something suspicious going on here."

Paula kept her eyes steady on me as she drank from her mug. "Yes, I saw all the police officers over at the neighbor's yesterday. Do you know what happened?"

I shifted in my seat, rubbing the side of my mug to warm up my fingers. "I'm not sure exactly. Someone mentioned at the inn that he'd passed away. They weren't sure if it was an accident or not, but I think the police are going to make a statement about it later today."

She gasped and pressed one of her hands against her lips. "Oh, no. What do you think happened to him? Do you think he was murdered?"

I shrugged. "Not sure. Like I said, the person I talked to didn't have many details." I chose not to mention the fact that my mother and I had been the ones to discover his body. That felt like a detail I should keep to myself while the killer was still out there.

"Oh, that's so awful. Hopefully the police can figure out what happened to him and help us all move on from this."

"Yes, let's hope so. You didn't notice anything yesterday? Did you hear anything coming from his house?"

She shook her head. "I spent most of the morning packing up boxes here, then met a friend for lunch in Holliston. I wonder if he had much family? It saddens me to think about all this death recently."

"I heard he and Kathleen used to fight about her roses encroaching on his garden. Did you ever talk to him?"

"No, never. I mean, maybe the occasional hello or goodbye if we passed each other, but I tended to stay inside, keeping an eye on Kathleen. When she did go out into her garden to work, I'd stay inside and clean. I don't really know anything about him."

I sat back in my seat, deflated. What had I expected—that Paula would've seen the killer fleeing Joseph's house yesterday? That was probably too much to hope for.

"Now that you bring this up," Paula said slowly, her gaze down on her tea. "It does make me wonder about Kathleen's death."

"What do you mean?"

"Well, I know I said before that she and Rebecca had had a volatile relationship for years. They didn't talk much, but Rebecca was insistent about her mother going into a nursing home. She said she was doing it for her mother's protection, but now with this other man dead... I have to wonder if she's involved in all of this. Maybe he saw something he wasn't supposed to, so she had to kill him."

"I've been wondering the same thing. I mean, I don't know if Rebecca was involved in her mother's death; but now that her neighbor is dead, too, it does raise some interesting questions." Such as, where was Rebecca when Joseph was killed yesterday? Had she ever talked to her mother's neighbor?

"Well, let's just hope that the police get this all cleared up soon. I don't mean to rush you out, but I do need to get back to packing. Was there anything else?"

I shook my head, took a final sip of my tea, and stood. "Thanks for talking with me. And good luck with packing. I'll see myself out."

I strode out of the house, my thoughts spinning. It might be time to go find Kathleen's daughter again and ask some questions about her mother's death. She hadn't wanted to talk to me much at her mother's funeral after it became clear that I was suspicious about something, and she'd probably be even less likely to talk to me now.

But the more I dug into Kathleen's death, the more obvious it became that there was something else going on here, and Rebecca had a few things to answer for. Had she been trying to force her mother out of her home? Had she gotten upset when Kathleen wouldn't leave, and forced her down those stairs? I should have probably left all this for the police to figure out, but with two people dead, was anyone else in danger? This killer needed to be stopped.

As I left Kathleen's, I glanced over at Cassie's house. Maybe she'd seen something at Joseph's place that would explain who had killed him. Since I was here, I may as well ask her.

"No, sorry," she said, once she answered the door and I explained what I was doing here. She had her baby propped on her hip, and a TV sounded from the room behind her. "I didn't know him very well. He always seemed like kind of a grump, though. I am sorry to hear he's dead. Makes me nervous to think about all my neighbors dying." She shivered as the thought passed through her.

"He mentioned to me that he always saw strange things going on in Kathleen's house, and that he could hear singing. Did you ever see or hear anything strange?"

She shook her head. "Not really. Like I said before, I'm pretty busy with my business and my little girl. Doesn't give me much time to overhear what's happening at the neighbor's."

"Right. What about Kathleen's roses? Apparently, they were encroaching on Joseph's garden, and he was upset about it. Did you know anything about that?"

She cracked a smile. "I'm not much of a gardener. I tend

to kill any plants that I try to bring into the house. That's why I stick to my onesies—you can't kill fabric."

"True." I shifted my weight between my feet. This wasn't getting me anywhere. "Did you ever meet Kathleen's daughter, Rebecca?"

"No, not officially, but I'd sometimes see her going into Kathleen's house. Actually, if you want to talk to someone shady, I'd look into her daughter's husband."

David's face flashed through my mind. "What do you mean?"

"I could hear them arguing sometimes, Kathleen's daughter and her husband, when they'd leave Kathleen's house. He always seemed to be berating her, and once, I heard him threaten to hit her if she didn't shut up about something. I don't know what they were arguing about, but I do know that you don't go around threatening your wife like that. He seems like a nasty character."

And I'd seen him get rough with his wife in town while I was shopping with my mom. The more I learned about this guy, the more I didn't like him at all. "Thanks," I said, stepping down from her porch after it was clear she didn't have anything else to share.

There were definitely some weird things going on between Kathleen, Rebecca, and David. Had they killed Kathleen? Were they also responsible for Joseph's death? Had David's anger finally taken over him, and he'd gone after two innocent people? I didn't love the idea of confronting two potential killers, but I needed to learn more about these two and whether they were involved in all this.

The only problem with trying to track down Rebecca and David to talk about Kathleen's death again was that I didn't know where to find them. I knew they lived on the opposite side of town from Kathleen, but it was the middle of a weekday so they weren't likely to be home right now. I had no idea what they did for work, though, or if I could even interrupt them during their workday. There was someone in town who I could call that would have the answers for me, though.

"Rebecca and David? Sure, I know where they work," Miriam said on the phone, after I explained what I was looking for. "They own that mechanic shop down on State Street. He's a mechanic, but he has a few guys who help him out, and she does the books. They've been running that place for, oh, about fifteen years at this point. I think they're thinking about retiring soon, actually."

"Miriam, you are a lifesaver," I said, scribbling down the address she fed me. "Your next meal at the bistro is on me."

"Anytime, darling. Just please be careful, okay? Detective Patel is about to give her statement to the press about the investigation into Kathleen's death, and if her killer is out there, they may not appreciate you sticking your nose into things."

"Don't worry, I'll be careful. Thanks!" I hung up and put my car into drive, peeling away from the curb and heading in the direction of the mechanic's shop.

I wasn't eager to confront David after the violence I'd seen from him with his wife in town, and what I'd learned about him from other people, but there'd likely be other workers at the shop and probably other customers. He wouldn't want to make a big scene in front of everyone, so I'd likely be safe.

I hadn't needed any maintenance on my car since moving to Pine Brook, so I hadn't been to this mechanic's shop yet. In fact, there was another mechanic's shop closer to the inn that Nick always went to, so I was probably more likely to use that one in the future. But Rebecca and David didn't need to know that.

I parked in the lot next to the office building and headed inside. The mechanic's shop was a large affair with multiple stalls, several already filled with cars in need of repair. Paper snowflakes hung from the ceiling.

Rebecca was on the phone at the front desk, taking notes as the person on the other end spoke. A bell above the door rang out, and she glanced over at my entrance. A large, lavishly-decorated tree stood in the corner of the office, and brightly-colored lights were strung up around the walls.

"Peter, let me call you back," she said into the phone, then set it down in its cradle and smiled at me. "Hi there. Having some car troubles?"

"Um, yes," I said, realizing that I hadn't come up with an excuse on the drive over here. Some detective I was! "My car has been making a weird ticking sound for the past couple weeks. Someone suggested I come by to get it looked at."

"Should be easy enough. Just fill out this form and my husband will take a look once he's done with his last appointment." She passed me a clipboard with a piece of paper on top, and I grabbed a pen from a cup on her desk.

Framed photos hung on the walls around the office, and I wandered around, checking them out, struggling to come up with another way to segue into a conversation with her. Most of the photos were of cars, though there were a few with Rebecca and David with other people. Kathleen was in a couple of the photos, as well. May as well start there.

"You're Kathleen's daughter, right?" I asked, turning back to the desk. "Rebecca, isn't that right? I'm so sorry for your loss."

"Thank you." She narrowed her eyes at me as she studied my face. "You were at her funeral, weren't you?"

I cleared my throat and nodded, trying to figure out how to get out of this one. "Yes. I'm sorry if I upset you. I was just trying to get to know Kathleen better."

"It's fine," she said, waving her hand flippantly, but a wall had shut down behind her eyes, and I didn't think she was likely to tell me much more about her mom. Her customer service skills had kicked in so she wasn't going to make me leave, but she wasn't going to be friendly about this visit.

"Did you hear about Kathleen's neighbor?" I asked, thinking maybe I could catch her off guard. "He was killed, too."

"Really? I had no idea. Gosh, that's so sad." She seemed genuinely surprised as she sat back in her seat, but she could've also been a very good liar.

"Did you know him?"

"Not really. I know Mom had issues with him because of her roses. But I can't imagine why anyone would want to kill him." She fiddled with a pen on her desk, her gaze thoughtful.

Just then, David entered the office. "Becks, I finished with that last car. Oh, sorry," he added once he realized I was in the office, too. "Did you need help with your car?" he asked me.

"David, this is Simone," Rebecca explained. "You remember, she was at Mom's funeral."

"Oh, right," he said, crossing his arms. He held a wrench in one hand, and his eyes were guarded. "Need help with your car?"

"Yes, it's been making a ticking sound. But I was just telling Rebecca here about the death of Kathleen's neighbor. His name was Joseph. Did you know him?"

"No," David said. "Why would I?"

"Well, I know you two were interested in Kathleen's house. I thought maybe you spent time talking to her neighbors, too."

"What exactly are you insinuating?" he asked, his voice low.

I took a step back, wanting to put some distance between us. "I'm not insinuating anything; I'm just curious to see what you know."

"Well, what I know is that you should stop sticking your nose in where it doesn't belong," he said, taking a step closer to me and swinging the wrench out to his side.

Rebecca stood from the desk. "David, please," she said, her voice stern, but her husband wouldn't listen. Her sleeves rode up her arms as she stood, and her wrists poked out, dark spots standing out against her pale skin.

My mouth went dry at the sight. I'd seen those dark spots at Kathleen's funeral, too. I hadn't thought anything about it then, but now, with David approaching, and after seeing him get angry with his wife in town, they looked much more menacing.

I set the clipboard down and slowly edged my way around David. "You know, I actually don't think my car needs any work right now. The ticking sound has basically disappeared."

"Yeah, I think it's probably best if you leave," David said, leering down at me, gripping the wrench tight by his side.

"David, please," Rebecca repeated, her voice wavering, but he wasn't listening.

I backed out of the office and hurried over to my car, tearing out of the parking lot before I had a chance to put on my seatbelt.

It wasn't clear to me if Rebecca or David knew Joseph, but those spots on Rebecca's arms sure looked like bruises.

And from the way David was approaching me with that threatening wrench in his hand, it wasn't such a stretch to believe that he might've attacked his mother-in-law when she wouldn't give up her house, especially since I'd already seen him get angry with his wife in town. He could definitely be a killer. I still didn't have any proof, though.

14

I drove back to the inn on autopilot, my hands shaking on the steering wheel. David's outburst had spooked me, but I didn't know what to do about it. Someone getting angry at his place of work because I was asking questions about his dead mother-in-law wasn't a crime. If I went to Detective Patel and told her what had happened, she likely would've gotten upset at me for snooping around Kathleen's death again, and maybe even wonder if David should press charges against me. Those charges probably wouldn't stick, but if I involved the police now, and David had a chance to tell his side of the story, I didn't know what could happen after that. But it didn't seem good for me or for the inn's reputation.

A few guests were seated in the front lobby, lounging on couches and armchairs while they flipped through books or scrolled on their phones. The front desk was empty, but I figured Tracy was likely in the back office again.

There was a pile of mail on the desk, and I flipped through the envelopes, most of them spam. I groaned as I came across another Christmas card, this one from Ron

Chapman, a lawyer in town and a good friend. I appreciated how many people wanted to send us well wishes this season, but all it really made me think about was how behind I was on sending out cards. How was I going to find the time to do it? I was too busy with this murder investigation and running the inn with Nadia gone, I hadn't even gotten around to decorating my own apartment.

Penny strolled out of the bistro a few minutes later, a couple ornaments in hand. She headed straight for the Christmas tree in the corner, studying all the angles of the tree before hanging up a snowman in a Hawaiian shirt and a small, stuffed hen.

"I think the tree might be full enough," I called across the lobby, cracking a smile to soften my tone.

Penny laughed and came over to the front desk. "You might be right, but I can't help myself. I found those in one of the back closets in the kitchen and had to put them up. I simply love this time of year!" She gave a little shimmy and clapped her hands together.

"Well, I'm glad one of us is in the holiday spirit. I still haven't put anything up in my apartment."

She brushed away my concerns with a flick of her wrist. "Don't worry, I'm sure you'll get around to it. I'm just bummed that Nadia isn't here to see how beautiful everything looks in town. She loves Christmas in Pine Brook."

Penny gave a little wave, then headed back to the bistro, leaving me to my thoughts. I was also bummed that Nadia wasn't here, but not for the same reason as Penny. Things hadn't completely fallen apart at the inn while she was on her cruise, but if she stayed away for much longer, the quality of our service might slip. I'd never realized how vital she was to the success of the inn, and I hoped she didn't decide to run off with Christos and spend the rest of her days on a Greek island.

"Simone! How are you, my dear?" Isabella sauntered over to the front desk with a flip of her dark hair. Somehow, even though it was pouring rain outside, she still managed to look glamorous in tight jeans and a royal blue sweater, a camel-colored trench coat keeping her dry.

"Not bad," I said with a smile, choosing to keep all the drama with this murder investigation to myself. The police were going to announce that Kathleen's death wasn't an accident shortly; I didn't need to go around town letting people know that I was investigating again. Maybe Isabella could distract me from getting down in the dumps about Nadia being away.

"Is Tracy in the back? I've got some flights I want her to take a look at." Isabella pulled out her phone and unlocked the device, scrolling through a few screens.

"I just got back, but I think so."

"Perfect." She slipped her phone back into her jeans' pocket—how she managed to fit anything into those pockets, I had no idea—then leaned across the countertop and cradled my hands in hers. Her skin was smooth and warm, in stark contrast to my chilly fingertips. "I wanted to thank you personally for agreeing to let Tracy go on this trip with me. I haven't had much time to travel recently, and I wasn't even sure if it was the right time to take this trip with her now, but we agreed that it was a good idea for our relationship. I know how important this inn is, and of course I want to make sure it's successful. I'm grateful you're so willing to let Tracy take this time off with me."

I tensed at her words, but tried to keep my smile neutral. "Of course. Time off is important, and Tracy has done so much for the Hemlock."

"I agree," she said with a wink, then she dropped my hands and stepped away from the desk. "I'll head on back and check on Tracy. See you later, darling." She waved goodbye and strode off to the office.

Once she was out of sight, my shoulders slumped forward and I let out a deep breath. So much for Isabella distracting me from getting down in the dumps about Nadia being away. While I was happy for Tracy and Isabella and their blossoming relationship, I was still anxious at the idea of Tracy being gone from the inn for so long. I'd felt like I'd barely had time to consider the prospect before I agreed to it, and as I thought about all the things I'd have to do myself with Tracy gone, the ball of dread that had formed in my stomach at the prospect kept growing.

She was a good friend, as well as an excellent employee, and she deserved this time off as much as anyone, but could I keep the inn running and successful on my own? I'd always had Tracy to rely on when things weren't going well, and I didn't know how I'd handle things once she was gone.

As I threw myself a pity party, wondering how I'd run the inn without Tracy's support, the inn's door opened, and this time Miles walked through. His eyes were wide behind his wireframe glasses and his mussed hair stood up straight from his head, but I was glad to see him walking around after his hip problems earlier in the week. I waved and called out his name, and he made a beeline for the front desk.

"Have you seen Estelle?" he asked, skipping right over any pleasantries.

I blinked once at the abrupt introduction, then shook my head. "I saw her earlier, but I've been gone for a while and just got back to the inn. Maybe she's in the bistro?"

Miles nodded, fumbling with his rain-soaked coat, his

eyes darting around, and made to walk towards the bistro. I held out a hand to stop him before he could get too far.

"Is everything okay?" I asked. He tended to be a nervous man, but his current fidgeting seemed more extreme than normal.

He sagged against the countertop, his head drooping down. "I'm not sure. I'm worried about her. She's been running around ever since Kathleen died, looking for a killer, even though the police said it was an accident. I know she's upset about Kathleen's death, but this doesn't seem like the best way to handle it. I worry that she's not properly grieving Kathleen and is avoiding what happened."

"She does seem very determined to find this killer, more determined than I've seen her with investigations in the past. What do you think is going on?"

"Well, when you get to a certain age, mortality is a hard thing to deal with. I know you're still a long way off from this, dear, so it's hard to understand at your age, but at a certain age, you reach a point where everyone around you, people you've known for decades, start dying. And that can be hard to handle. Estelle and I are lucky that we have made it through so much together, but it's hard to see the people around you getting sick and not faring as well. I think that's what's happening here."

"I understand. I didn't quite think about it that way."

"And as you know, Estelle and Kathleen were close. Not the best of friends, of course, but still very close. Probably closer than you realize. Kathleen wasn't much older than us when she died. She was starting to show her age, too. She couldn't get around as easily as she used to. I'm worried about Estelle looking for a killer who might not even exist. It's a hard thing to reconcile, the loss of a friend, and I think Estelle is getting worried about what might happen to her.

You know all about my hip, of course. I think Estelle is scared but is distracting herself with this investigation."

I reached out and patted Miles' hand. "I hadn't realized she might be worried about her own mortality, too. I do think you're right that she's not grieving Kathleen's death properly. I'm just not sure how to get her to stop for a moment and process what happened."

"Estelle is very determined, but at some point, she'll have to slow down."

"How is your hip, by the way? I'm glad to see you moving around."

"Thanks, dear. I'm doing better. Not yet at one hundred percent, and I think that might be contributing to Estelle getting so focused on what happened to Kathleen. I think she's having trouble facing the possibility of me being hurt, too. Still, I appreciate you looking out for her and for checking on me. I'll go see if she's in the bistro. If you hear from her, will you let her know I'm looking for her?" Miles smiled sadly, then walked away towards the bistro.

I propped an elbow on the countertop and rested my chin in my palm, thinking about what Miles had said. I'd thought that Estelle was so determined to find Kathleen's killer because she was having trouble grieving the loss of her friend. If Kathleen's death had been an accident due to her getting unsteady on her feet, then Estelle might've had to start thinking about whether she or Miles could slip and fall at some point. That was a hard thing to consider.

Still, Estelle might have been right that Kathleen was murdered. Once the police officially announced that they were launching an investigation, Estelle would likely feel vindicated and even more determined to find the killer. After my run-in with Kathleen's daughter and son-in-law, I had a feeling they might've played a role in Kathleen's death, but I lacked proof and I didn't know how to go about getting it.

If I kept snooping around, maybe I'd be able to find the truth about what happened to Kathleen and help my friend get the closure she needed to move forward from Kathleen's death.

Miles came out of the bistro a few minutes later, letting me know that Estelle wasn't in there, and reminding me to tell her he was looking for her when I saw her next. I promised to call him once I heard from her, and he dragged himself back out into the rainstorm.

A couple guests had some questions for me about their rooms and the spa, so I spent the next few hours helping them out and dealing with other inn business. When five o'clock rolled around, I got a notification on my phone that the Pine Brook Police Department was holding a press conference. Keeping the volume low on my phone so as not to freak out any guests that might be hanging around, I turned on the press conference and watched Detective Patel make her statement.

"After some new evidence has come out, we are revising our original statement that Kathleen Richard's death was an accident. We are now treating her death as suspicious and will be launching an investigation into the circumstances surrounding her death."

The room Patel was in burst into a chorus of voices as the various journalists and concerned citizens who had attended the press conference began peppering her with questions. Patel held up a hand to quiet the crowd and leaned back down to the microphone.

"At this time, we will not be taking questions as we initiate our investigation. I'll be back tomorrow with another update once I have more to share. Thank you."

With that, she turned and strode away from the microphone, even as more questions were thrown her way.

The video transitioned back to a local news station, the blonde newscaster seated behind a desk summarizing what Patel had said for anyone who was just tuning in. It wasn't likely that this newscaster would have any other information than what Patel had already said, so I turned off the broadcast and put my phone away, replaying the statement in my head.

Given the rumor mill in Pine Brook, it didn't seem like a great idea to make a statement like that and then not take any questions to answer the questions inevitably flying around town now, but Patel was likely inundated with work for the investigation and probably didn't have much time to spend with journalists right now. Still, I had to wonder about what kind of shockwaves this update was sending through the community.

This question was at least partially answered a short while later, when Louise, Kathleen's close friend, poked her head through the inn doors and glanced around. She spotted me at the front desk and beelined straight for me.

"Louise," I said, straightening up. "I'm surprised to see you here." After her sudden departure at Kathleen's funeral, I hadn't expected to see the woman again any time soon. I didn't think she was a killer, but her suspicious behavior had me thinking she was hiding something, and if she knew I was looking into Kathleen's death, she'd probably want to keep her distance.

"Do you have a minute to talk?" she asked, clutching her purse tightly to her chest. "I'm sorry for interrupting you while you're working, but I needed to tell you this right away."

"Of course. What's going on?"

"I heard on the news that the police are investigating Kathleen's death. They think someone killed her! I know you were asking questions about her at her funeral, and I know you've solved crimes like this in the past. I didn't want to leave you with the wrong impression."

"What do you mean?"

She leaned forward, lowering her voice. "I know I acted strangely at Kathleen's funeral, when I ran off like that. It was very rude of me, but I felt overwhelmed with all the questions, and I didn't want to admit the truth."

"I'm sorry for overwhelming you like that. I didn't mean to make you upset. What didn't you want to admit?"

She sighed, her gaze down, her knuckles paper white where she gripped her purse. "I didn't kill Kathleen, I swear, but I do have a secret, and Kathleen knew about it... I've got a gambling problem. A big one. I-I gambled away a lot of money recently, playing the slot machines. Kathleen and I got into a fight about it, a few days before her death. Over the years, she'd tried to get me help, tried to talk me out of what I was doing, but I wouldn't ever listen. Finally, it got so bad that I might lose my house. Kathleen was just trying to help me, but we ended up yelling at each other at her house. I was worried you'd learn about our fight and think that I killed her to keep her quiet, so that's why I ran away. But I promise, I didn't do it."

"Oh, Louise, I'm so sorry." I squeezed her hand reassuringly. "I don't think you killed her, but it does sound like you need help. What are you going to do about your house?"

"I know. I think I've finally reached that rock bottom that people are always talking about. I reached out to a support group and my bank, and I'm going to get help. But once I saw that the police are looking for Kathleen's killer, I remembered how I acted before, and I wanted to make sure you knew what had really happened. Kathleen was a good friend, and I'm so sad she's gone." Louise's eyes filled with tears, and I passed her a tissue from a box on the front desk.

"I appreciate you coming to talk to me. I don't think you killed her, but I do wonder if you might know anything about who did. I'm starting to wonder if Rebecca and David might've had something to do with her death. I know they're interested in selling her house, and it seems like David has a bit of a temper. Do you think it's possible they killed her?"

Louise cocked her head to the side, her mouth pursed as she thought. "Well, I suppose anything is possible. I do know that David seems like a bad guy. Kathleen didn't like him at all. She was worried about Rebecca and if she was safe with him."

The bruises on Rebecca's wrists that I'd seen at Kathleen's funeral flashed through my mind, as did the fight I'd seen between David and Rebecca in town. Was David hurting Rebecca, and had he hurt her mother, too?

"Thanks for coming down here. I'll let you know if I learn anything else about Kathleen's killer."

Louise nodded her thanks, then turned around and left the inn. I leaned my hip against the countertop as I thought about what she'd told me, then I pulled up the search bar on my computer and typed in the name of Kathleen's neighbor's online shop and first name. I found a Facebook page with a phone number listed, which I dialed.

"Onesies & Twosies," the neighbor said when she picked up.

"Hi, Cassie, this is Simone Evans, from the Hemlock Inn."

"Oh, hi, Simone. What can I do for you? Are you interested in a onesie?"

"No, but I did have a question for you. Do you recall ever

seeing Kathleen's daughter or son-in-law hanging around with Joseph next door? Did they ever talk to him?"

"Hmm, no, not that I can remember. I did sometimes see Paula, her nurse, talking with him. I think they were discussing Kathleen's roses. But I don't think they knew each other very well or anything."

Something sparked in my brain at her words. "Really? Paula told me she'd never spoken to him before."

"They weren't very long conversations. I wouldn't consider them friendly or anything, at least as far as I could tell. Paula probably just thought she was helping out Kathleen as part of her job since Joseph always complained about her roses."

"That makes sense. What about his peanut allergy? Did you know about that?"

"I do remember hearing about that. He was always so particular with what he ate because of it."

"Did other people in town know about it?" Was it possible Rebecca and David had found out and used it to kill him?

"I'm not sure about that. He didn't go around town talking about it, as far as I could tell."

"Got it. Well, thanks for your time." We said our goodbyes, and I hung up the phone, my thoughts whirling in my head.

Paula had said she'd never talked to Joseph, but would she have counted a brief conversation about roses in that statement? Maybe she did just consider that part of her job and not worth mentioning. Was there anything else she'd told me that wasn't the complete truth, too?

I'd been hoping that Cassie would tell me that Rebecca and David had known Joseph well, and that they knew about his peanut allergy. Still, Kathleen had known about it, and maybe she'd mentioned it to her daughter at some point. If Joseph had figured out that Rebecca and David had murdered Kathleen, they could've snuck into his house and put ground peanuts into some of his food, or forced him to eat it. Two people were more likely able to force another person to do something like that, and David was a big guy. That, combined with the bruises on Rebecca's wrists and the fight I'd seen, had me convinced that David was a violent killer. But I still needed more proof.

15

The next day, I woke up to someone knocking on my front door, much earlier than was appropriate. I groaned and rolled over, ready to ignore them, but the knocking wouldn't stop. With a sigh, I climbed out of bed and stomped through my apartment, my energy deflating once I looked through the peephole and saw Estelle on the other side.

"Do you know what time it is?" I asked, swinging open the door and rubbing my eyes.

"It's never too early to hunt for a killer," she said, squeezing past me and walking into my apartment.

"Come on in," I muttered, shutting the door and following her into the kitchen.

Estelle began pulling out the makings for coffee, switching on my coffee machine and grabbing beans from the cupboard. I yawned and trailed after her, taking a seat on a barstool.

"You seem very alert this morning," I said, narrowing my eyes at her as she hummed her way through making me a cup of coffee.

"I'm sure you heard the news," she said over her shoulder, her attention on the coffee machine. "The police are finally investigating Kathleen's death as a murder. I knew I was right."

I'd considered calling her after Patel's press conference to discuss the announcement, but I'd remembered what Miles had said about Estelle not processing Kathleen's death. I didn't want to encourage her investigative tendencies right now.

"Have you talked to your husband?" I asked instead, gratefully accepting the mug of coffee she set before me.

She nodded and began washing the dishes I'd left sitting in my sink last night. "Of course. We had dinner together. His hip is doing much better."

"Did he tell you anything important? Like, 'stop investigating your friend's murder'?"

Estelle scoffed and smirked at me from the sink. "You know that man never thinks I should investigate murders. Why would this be any different?"

I took a sip of coffee and held back a groan. Estelle could really make a good cup of this stuff. "I just know that he's worried about you. You should listen to what he has to say."

"I know he is." She finished stacking the last dish on the dish rack to dry, then leaned back against the countertop and faced me. "And I think I've been doing a very good job of keeping away from suspects this time around. In fact, I thought you were taking the lead on this case, but you didn't even tell me that the police were going to start investigating. I thought we were partners?"

I winced at her remonstrating. I hated disappointing people. "I'm sorry for not saying anything sooner, but Detective Patel asked me to keep quiet until her press conference.

Then Miles talked to me and said he was worried about you, and I didn't want to do anything to interfere in your marriage. I'm just worried about you. It's okay to grieve for your friend."

Estelle let out a deep exhale. "I'll grieve once her killer is caught. And don't worry, you're not interfering. Now, please, tell me what you've learned."

I took another big gulp of coffee to give myself a moment to get my thoughts together. Estelle was still letting this murder investigation get in the way of grieving her friend's death. Was I just encouraging her avoidant behavior by updating her on my progress? I knee Estelle wasn't going to give up until the killer was caught, no matter what I said.

Resigned, I launched into what I'd learned over the past couple of days. Estelle's eyes widened as I gradually made the argument that I suspected David of murder and potentially spousal abuse.

"I knew it! I always knew he was a bad guy. I can't believe he would hurt his wife like that. What's our next step?"

"Well, I'd like to go back to sleep for another hour, but after this cup, I think I'm officially awake. I've got some paperwork to take care of at the inn, and you should go back to your husband. Does he even know you're gone?"

"Don't worry, he's always up before me. And I told him where I was going so he wouldn't worry."

"Good. David could be very dangerous, so you need to stay out of this for now. We should let the police handle this."

"You can't be serious! Now is not the time to stop your investigation. The police can only do so much. You know how easily people talk to you—I bet you can get the killer to confess before they do."

I pursed my lips in annoyance. After Patel's press conference, I'd hoped that Estelle would agree we should leave this to the police. I shouldn't have been too surprised that my friend still wanted to snoop.

"All right, fine, I'll keep digging around and see what I can find." I also had a little nugget in my brain that kept reminding me that Paula had lied about knowing Joseph. It might've just been a slip on her part, the kind of thing you might not think was important to mention, but I had to wonder if she'd acted like she hadn't spoken to him for some other reason.

"Go back to your husband," I repeated. "Even if he is feeling better, I'm sure he wants to know you're safe, too. I've got this handled."

"All right, fine, I'll go home and spend the day with my husband. But please keep me updated." Estelle pulled me into a tight hug, then dashed out of my apartment, hopefully heading back home and not going after a killer.

Everything was getting so complicated with this case. I was glad the police were finally taking the investigation seriously, but had too much time passed for there to still be evidence for them to find? I knew I was getting close to the answer, but I needed more proof before I could bring anything back to Patel; otherwise, she'd just kick me out of the police station again.

I finished getting ready for the day, then climbed the stairs to Nick's apartment and knocked on his door. I hadn't heard from him in a few days, and I wanted to see how he was doing. I also wanted to bring up the idea of us moving in together. With the threat of a killer running loose in town, and my mom's questions about where our relationship was going, it seemed time to get on the same page with him.

It was still early, but he also tended to get up early before heading to the farm, and I hoped to talk to him about everything that was going on.

No answer to my knock. Had he already left for the farm? I knocked again, but still no answer. I turned around and left the apartment building, sending him a text message to check in. Hopefully he'd call me later and we could talk.

To my surprise, I found Nick at the inn, speaking with my mother in the corner of the lobby. A smile blossomed across my face as I strode over to them.

"Hey there," I said once I was within sight.

My mom jumped back in surprise, her eyes wide, while Nick smiled and pulled me into a hug. "Hey, you," he said, kissing my forehead. "I was talking to your mom about her practice down in L.A. Seems pretty cool."

"Yes, it's pretty impressive." I glanced over at my mom, but her gaze was down on her nails, studying her manicure.

"Hey, listen," I said, turning back towards Nick and lowering my voice. "I'm glad I caught you. I wanted to talk to you about something. About...plans for us, maybe. Do you have some time to talk?"

Nick's eyes widened briefly, then his face shifted back to a smile, and he gave me another kiss. "I'd love to talk, but I've actually got to get back to the farm. Um, why don't we talk later? I'll text you." He gave me a hug and patted my mom's shoulder goodbye, then rushed out of the inn.

Strange that he'd be at the Hemlock talking to my mom about her practice, then rush off to the farm as soon as I showed up. Maybe he'd been dropping off produce in the kitchen and gotten caught up in conversation with her.

"What a lovely man," my mother said, pulling my attention back to her. "And can I just say, this inn is truly magical," she said with a dreamy smile. "I haven't slept this good in months!"

"I'm glad to hear it. I'm sorry I've been so absent recently. There's been a lot going on right now."

"Don't even worry about it. I'm just glad I get a chance to see you for a bit. Sylvia would be so proud of you. I took a stroll around the back of the inn last night before it got dark, just to see how far back the property stretched. You know that creek that runs through the woods? Do you remember when Chrissy fell into the creek that summer by accident, soaking all her clothes?" She laughed at the memory.

I held my hand to my mouth to stifle a chuckle. "Oh gosh, I'd forgotten about that. Poor Aunt Sylvia came out with an armful of towels, but Chrissy had already run into the lobby, fretting about ruining her new sneakers. She'd tracked water everywhere!"

"But to her credit, Sylvia didn't freak out."

"Yup. Cool as a cucumber. We had some good times back then."

"Sure did," she said wistfully.

Now seemed as good a time as any to bring up the question that had been brewing on my mind all week. "You two used to be close, Mom. Please tell me what happened between you to change that. What did Aunt Sylvia mean in her letter about a fight?"

At those words, my mom's eyes shuttered, the nostalgic laughter on her face disappearing. "I don't know why you keep bringing up that letter. It's not important at all."

"I'm just trying to understand why we weren't close to her anymore. She made such a great life for herself, and I wish I could've seen more of it when she was alive."

"Well, it doesn't matter now, and it's best if you just leave it alone. Stop asking me about it." With those words, she turned around and stalked back up the stairs to her room.

I let out a deep breath once she was gone. Wow. Where

had all that come from? I hadn't realized I was going to set her off so badly by asking about the letter again. What had happened between the two women that would make my mom so tense like this?

"Hey, Simone!" Hank appeared at my side, causing me to jump in surprise at his sudden appearance.

"Jeez, Hank, you scared me," I said.

The chef had the good grace to blush and smile ruefully. "Sorry about that. There's a lull in the kitchen, so I wanted to come by and see how you were doing. You've had a busy few days, right? With your mom visiting and everything?"

And with my mom yelling at me, plus a murder investigation, yes, it had been a busy few days. But I kept my thoughts to myself. "Yes, things have been busy. How's the kitchen?"

"Pretty good," he said, bobbing his head. "Javier has been a great help. He's been making some of his own dishes, too. Maybe in the new year, we can start featuring a Javier-specific menu."

"That's a good idea," I said, even though my mind had drifted back to my mom and her outburst.

It was hard to focus on the minutiae of the inn, knowing that my mom was holding onto a pain from the past that she couldn't talk about. It must've been hard to be back at the Hemlock with the memory of their tense relationship on her mind. Should I give up on my quest to find the truth? Sylvia had told me to ask her about it, though. As painful as it might be for my mom, I couldn't help myself from wanting to know what had happened between them.

"Tracy was telling me all about her trip," Hank went on. "It sounds pretty amazing. I can't believe she's going to be gone for so long!"

"Yeah, me either," I said, my shoulders drooping at the

idea of running this place without her. Why did it feel like everyone was abandoning me when I really needed them?

"I was talking with someone from Pine Brook in the bistro earlier, and they were asking if I made pies for birthday parties or other events. They loved my pie during the pie contest in the spring, and they were willing to pay me to make them a pie. A couple other people overheard and said they'd be interested, too. Maybe I should look into starting a catering business on the side for my pies. Since Javier's helping out more in the kitchen, I've got more time to spare. What do you think?"

I snapped back to attention, my thoughts still focused on wondering how I'd possibly run the inn without Tracy. "Hmm? A catering business? Uh, yeah, that sounds cool. Um, sorry Hank, but I'm a little tired right now. Do you mind if we talk about this later?"

"No problem. You should get some rest. I better get back there. See you later!" Hank waved goodbye cheerfully, my lukewarm response to his catering business idea not seeming to bother him, then sauntered back to the kitchen.

I sighed and rested against the countertop. The lobby was quiet, which meant my ruminations finally had space to fill up my head. There was one thing I liked to do whenever my mind was spiraling like this. I set up the little sign at the front desk, letting guests know to ring the bell if they needed service—someone from the bistro or back office would come help them—then went to the staff bathroom and changed into a pair of running clothes I kept onsite for just such a moment. Running was something that always helped to clear my mind, and right now, I felt like I really needed it.

It wasn't raining, but it was cold outside, so I made sure to put on a thermal top and pants and added mittens to my outfit. I began a slow jog away from the inn, my feet pounding against the pavement. A car started up behind me in the inn's parking lot, and I moved to the side of the street to give them space to go around me.

However, the car didn't pass. I glanced over my shoulder, seeing a large, black truck with darkened windows, creeping along behind me. I slowed my run and moved over to where the pavement turned to grass, getting off of the road completely. Sometimes big cars felt like they needed more space to get around runners, and I didn't want to get in the way.

Rather than move around me, the truck sped up and the driver drove the truck off the side of the road, coming straight at me!

I FORCED myself further into the underbrush, trying to get out of the way of the truck's path, and tripped over a root. My body flew through the air and deeper into the woods that lined the road just outside of the inn. I landed flat on my face and groaned, trying to pick myself up as the truck's engine still revved behind me. At that moment, two other cars came over the hill from the opposite direction, approaching the inn. The truck's revving died down, then the driver hit the gas and sped off.

I was too far into the woods for the two cars that had gone past to realize I was back here. I managed to flip myself onto my back and stared up at the sky, watching small snowflakes begin to drift down from the gray clouds. I didn't even feel the cold as they landed on me.

This was not the first time I'd been run off the road by a

car while out for a run. Maybe it meant I should stop running altogether.

What it definitely meant was that Kathleen and Joseph's killer thought I was getting too close to the truth and wanted to do something about it.

16

"And did you get a good look at the truck?"

I sighed and pushed a curl of hair off my face, wincing as I moved my arm a little too aggressively. "As I've said, three times now, all I could see was that it was big and black. The windows were darkened, too, so I couldn't see inside."

Officer Collins stared at me over the top of his ancient computer, then he typed a few notes onto the keyboard.

I was at the Pine Brook Police Department, reporting my attempted murder to the appropriate authorities, but not getting much out of the interaction. The bullpen was almost empty, all of the other cops probably out investigating Kathleen's death—as they should be, finally—so I was stuck with Officer Collins, who always looked like he thought I was lying to his face.

I leaned across Collins' desk. "Is Detective Patel around? I think she'd want to know about what happened to me."

Collins typed a few more words into his computer, not looking up from the keyboard. I opened my mouth, ready to repeat my question in case he hadn't heard me, when he looked up and spoke. "Detective Patel is out working on a case. I'll be sure to share this report with her when she returns."

I had a feeling my report might get tossed into the trash as soon as I left, but I held back a sarcastic retort. Collins was my only way to get through to Patel since she wasn't answering my texts or phone calls, so it was best if I played nice. "I believe that my attack has something to do with the case that Detective Patel is working on. If you'd just get her on the phone, I'm sure she'd want to hear about this."

Collins' attention was back on his keyboard, and I sighed and leaned back in my seat, looking around the empty bullpen. This was getting me nowhere, and the owner of that truck was probably fleeing town as we spoke.

"And where were you running when this truck allegedly tried to attack you?"

I rolled my eyes. "There's nothing *alleged* about it—I was attacked by a truck on the road leading from the Hemlock Inn. You should get someone out there to check for tire tracks or something."

Collins peered at me, his gaze blank. "Cars go fast down that road, and the visibility is poor coming over that hill. Maybe you shouldn't run up there anymore."

I huffed and crossed my arms over my chest. This was getting me nowhere. I'd have better luck searching for this truck myself.

I tensed in my seat, wondering if Collins could sense my thoughts. Maybe it wasn't such a bad idea for me to go looking for that truck. I mean, it was a pretty bad idea, but since Patel was nowhere to be found and Collins clearly wished he could go back to staring at his phone—which is what he'd been doing when I'd shown up to report the attack—maybe I should see what I could figure out about the truck and who had come after me on my own.

"Is that all?" I asked Collins, already getting antsy to do my own investigating.

Collins shrugged and typed a couple more keys on his computer. "Sure. Just let me print this and have you sign it." We sat in silence as his ancient printer printed out the statement, then he passed it to me along with a pen, and I scribbled my name on the bottom.

"Thanks for all your help," I said, unable to hide a hint of sarcasm from creeping into my words.

"We're here to protect and serve," Collins droned monotonously, his attention back on his phone. I rolled my eyes and walked away. I sure felt protected right now.

I hurried out of the police station and dashed across the parking lot to my car. Once inside, I turned on the heat to warm myself up but paused before leaving to give myself a moment to think. I didn't have the resources to go after a suspected hit and run perpetrator, but if I could remember something more about that truck, maybe I could track it down myself.

Like I'd told Collins, all I'd mostly seen was something big and black and scary. The windows had been tinted, so I couldn't see a driver or even the shape of one. I shut my eyes, taking a few deep breaths and bringing my attention back to that moment on the road when I looked back and realized the truck was following after me. Was there anything distinct about it? Anything I could use to figure out who owned it?

My eyes popped open, and I sat straight up in my seat. I did remember seeing another big, black truck recently—at Rebecca and David's mechanic's shop. It had been one of several cars parked in the garage. I couldn't be certain that it was the same truck, but it made sense that David might try to come after me now. I'd told a few different people that I suspected him of murder, and if it had gotten back to him or Rebecca somehow, they may have decided their best option was to eliminate me completely.

The truck I'd seen at the garage hadn't looked like one they used regularly since it was parked between a couple other junkers. There had also been two cars parked close to the office that likely belonged to David and Rebecca. This truck might've been an extra one they were working on, like the other junkers I saw. David wouldn't have wanted to use a truck that was registered in his name to come after me.

I put my car in drive and pulled out of the parking lot, heading back towards the inn. There wasn't much I could do about it now since I wasn't ready to confront Rebecca or David about whether they'd attacked me with a truck. Plus, I didn't have any proof that the truck belonged to them or to their shop. However, if I could get another look at that shop, maybe I could find the truck and confirm that it had been used to come after me today.

I couldn't go now, though. It was barely two o'clock, and they'd be working. However, I could wait until later, once I knew the shop was closed, and see what I could find then since they likely didn't move the cars inside at night. There were a lot of windows around the outside of the shop, so maybe I could peek my head through the window and spot the truck inside. There was always the possibility that David had gotten rid of it as soon as he drove away from the crime scene, but I didn't have a lot of other options right now. I'd go back to the mechanic's shop after hours, once it was dark, and see what I could find.

I SAT in my car across from the mechanic's shop later that night, shivering in my seat. It was almost below freezing outside, but I didn't want to turn on my engine and draw attention to myself or wear out the battery. The mechanic's shop was quiet across the street, but I was waiting until I was certain that no one was inside before sneaking around the back to snoop through the windows.

After leaving the police station, I'd spent the rest of the afternoon helping out with guests at the inn, booking appointments for the spa, folding towels, and calling Patel's cell phone whenever I had a free moment. She still wasn't answering, and I was getting nervous about who out there might want to kill me.

As soon as I had a minute alone, I called Nick to tell him what had happened. "I'm all right, I promise," I had said quickly, once his voice had taken on a hysterical tone at my news. "I reported it to the police, and they'll keep an eye out for the truck." I didn't add that I had a sneaking suspicion that Officer Collins might've tossed out my report as soon as I left the station.

Nick had sighed, his concern for me radiating through the phone line. "Well, as long as the police are looking into it, I guess there's not much more you can do... Just be careful, okay? I don't know what I'd do if anything happened to you. I love you."

We said our goodbyes after that, my cheeks warming at his kind words. Nick really cared about me, and I was being silly by hesitating about us moving in together. It hadn't felt like the time to bring it up on the phone, after telling him about my near-death experience, but as soon as we had a few minutes alone, I was going to ask him.

My mom didn't come down from her room, or at least I didn't see her pass through the lobby. It was going to be an awkward few weeks together if we didn't make up soon, unless she was planning on going back to Los Angeles after our fight. I hadn't expected her reaction when I'd brought up Sylvia's letter again, and I had a feeling her outburst meant there was more to the story than she was telling me.

I didn't want her to leave without talking about what had happened between her and Sylvia, but I wasn't quite ready to confront her and get yelled at again. It was probably best if I gave her some space right now, as she was clearly still upset about whatever had happened between her and Sylvia all those years ago. I didn't want to push her too far.

Estelle had called in the afternoon, looking for an update on the case. I kept things vague, only telling her that I was still looking into some proof that David had killed Kathleen, but that I thought I was getting close. I didn't tell her about my attack, as I knew she'd come down to the inn and try to figure out who had done it. I wanted to keep her safe, so I thought it best if she didn't know about what happened. Of course, instead that meant that I was now about to snoop around a potential killer's place of work all alone, without my trusty sidekick by my side.

I'd been sitting in my car for almost thirty minutes, and my fingers were starting to cramp up from the cold. No sound or movement had come from the mechanic's shop in the time that I'd been sitting out front, so I hoped that meant no one was there. I took a few deep breaths to try to calm my mind and pump myself up for what I was about to do, then climbed out of my car and crossed the street to the shop.

I'd changed into dark jeans and a dark jacket when I went home, hoping that this would help me blend in with my surroundings. There were several security lights around the perimeter of the shop, so I wasn't in as much darkness as I'd planned for.

The mechanic's shop was on a lonely street in Pine Brook, the nearest house or business two or three blocks away, so I didn't think anyone would stumble onto me and see what I was doing in the light. Still, I kept my movements furtive and dashed around to the back, out of sight of the lights and anyone walking past the building.

I kept my eyes peeled for security cameras that might alert someone to my presence, but I didn't see anything that looked like a camera on the outside of the building.

Several cars were parked in the back lot, in various states of repair. One had its hood removed, another was missing a few tires, and a third had what I could only describe as its guts hanging out the front of it. No big black truck, though.

I tiptoed to the back door, skirting around the windows. If someone was inside the shop, I didn't want them to see me back here. From the side, I leaned out and looked through one of the windows. More cars were parked inside, but the lights were off, and I couldn't actually make out the color or model of the cars. There might've been a truck in the last row, but I couldn't tell from where I was standing.

"What are you doing here?"

I jumped out of my skin at the sound of someone's voice, letting out a cry. Spinning around, I faced Rebecca. Her hands were on her hips as she stared me down.

"Well?" she said after a moment, when I didn't speak.

"I, um, I was in the area, and thought I heard something back here. Sounded like a raccoon."

Rebecca furrowed her brow, my excuse not coming across as super believable. "A raccoon? So you decided to look through our windows?"

"I thought maybe it had snuck inside, so I was just

checking—"

"Save it," she said, cutting me off and pulling out her phone. "I'm calling the police. They can deal with your story."

"Wait," I said, reaching out to stop her. "Where were you this afternoon?"

She stilled. "I was here. Why?"

"Where was David?"

She shrugged. "I don't know. He went out for a few hours. What's that got to do with anything?"

"I was nearly run over by a big, black truck this afternoon, and I think your husband was driving it."

Rebecca paled at my words. "That...that's not possible. He-he wouldn't do that."

"Really? Just like he wouldn't cause those bruises on your arm, or kill your mother?"

Her eyes widened and she took a step back from me, holding her hands protectively against her chest. "I-I don't know what you're talking about."

I took a step closer, holding my hands up to let her know I wasn't going to hurt her. "I saw the bruises, Rebecca. How long has he been hitting you?"

She shook her head rapidly, some locks of hair escaping her ponytail and floating down around her face as her eyes filled with tears. "It's not like that," she stammered, her voice wavering. "He loves me!"

"Someone who loves you wouldn't hurt you like that," I said slowly, taking a couple more cautious steps towards her. "Please, just tell me what's going on. I want to help you."

At those words, Rebecca burst into tears, collapsing onto herself as the truth came out. I reached out and grabbed her before she had a chance to fall, holding her against me as she sobbed.

17

A few minutes later, we were seated inside Rebecca's office. She had a small kettle and hotplate in the corner, so I made her a cup of tea and passed it to her. Her hands trembled as she held the Styrofoam.

"Rebecca, what's going on? I saw the fight you two got into a couple days ago in town. Kathleen knew about his abuse, didn't she? That's why you two were always fighting? Kathleen wouldn't want to see you hurting like this."

There was a pause after I finished speaking, the silence in the office practically deafening. I opened my mouth to say something else, anything else to convince her to talk to me, when she finally spoke.

"It started years ago, not long after we got married." She took a tiny sip of the tea. "He was so nice, at first. He seemed like a great husband. I-I was a nervous child, always jumping at everything, afraid to do anything. I never thought I'd find love. Then David came into my life, and it was like he really saw me. I fell in love so fast."

I stayed silent as she paused and took another drink,

worried that if I said anything, I might spook her from talking.

She let out a tiny sigh and seemed to relax more into her seat. "Things got bad a couple years after we got married. I, um, I can't have kids, and David, he-he didn't like that." She looked down, tears falling down her cheeks, ashamed. "We tried everything to get pregnant, but it just wasn't working. One day, I suggested adoption—I just wanted a child, I didn't care how we got them. That was the first time he hit me."

I flinched at her words, my heart breaking at this poor woman who just wanted to start a family and instead got this treatment.

"Why didn't you leave?" I asked. I thought I already knew the answer to this question, but I figured I may as well ask it.

She smiled through her tears, raising one shoulder dejectedly. "Why doesn't any woman leave? I didn't think I could do better. This shop is in his name, and so is our house. I figured he'd tell some judge that I was flighty or irresponsible and not deserving of spousal support. Or maybe he'd do something worse, and not let me leave."

"Did Kathleen know?" I asked again.

"She suspected, but I never came out and said it. But she could tell, just in the way David spoke to me when he thought we were alone. Over the years, he got more comfortable showing his true colors around my mom, and she got more upset with how he was treating me. I didn't want her to have to see that all that time, so I pulled away from her. It seemed like every time I talked to her, it just led to us fighting about him. We used to be so close, and now she's gone..." Her voice trailed off as another round of sobs wracked her body, her hands shaking.

I reached out and grabbed her cup, setting it on the desk between us to keep it from spilling. I gently took her hands in mine, softly rubbing at her fingers. "Rebecca, I want to help you. Please, let me help you. I know someone at the police station who can get you out of this situation. You don't deserve to be treated like this."

She looked up at me, her eyes red and raw from crying. "I don't think I can live without him," she said softly, her voice barely above a whisper. "How can I go on without him, now that my mother is dead, too?"

I squeezed her hand gently. "I believe in you. You're a strong woman, and you don't deserve to live like this anymore. Kathleen wouldn't want you to live like this. You might not be able to make up with her anymore, but you can still save yourself. Please, let me help you."

She didn't say anything for a moment, but she didn't pull away from me, either. After a few seconds of silence, she nodded, and I pulled her into a hug.

"Where is David right now?" I asked.

"At home. I stayed late tonight to get some paperwork done, but I also just wanted to have some time away from him," Rebecca explained. "He's probably passed out in front of the TV right now. What if he figures out what I'm doing?"

"He won't figure it out, don't worry. I'll make sure you're protected." I dialed Detective Patel's number again and huffed out a breath of exasperation when her voicemail picked up for the second time. Where was she?

"Do you think I should stay here?" Rebecca asked. She gnawed on a fingernail, her toe tapping out a beat on the concrete floor. "What if he decides to come back to get one of his tools or something?"

"You're right." I dropped my phone into my purse and stood. "Let's get out of here while I try to get ahold of someone who can help. We can go back to my apartment and wait there until we know what to do next."

I led Rebecca out of the mechanic's shop, keeping an eye out for any sound that we weren't alone. It would've been quite a coincidence for David to show up on the night his wife was leaving him and reporting his abuse to the police, but stranger things could happen. Now that I was involved in this, I couldn't let anything happen to her.

I bundled Rebecca up into my car and headed in the direction of my apartment, tapping my fingers against the steering wheel as I thought about what to do next. Patel wasn't answering my calls, and I didn't know who would be at the police station right now, especially since most of the cops in town were out investigating Kathleen's death. I worried that if Chief Tate or another grumpy cop were at the station, they might not listen to Rebecca's story. I could only keep her safe at my apartment for so long, before David started looking for her again.

Rebecca's voice cut through the silence, interrupting my thoughts. "Thank you for doing this. I-I know we don't know each other very well, but I'm so grateful for your help."

I sent her a smile, tightening my hands on the steering wheel. "Of course. I just want to keep you safe. We'll find a way out of this, don't worry."

Lola came to greet us when we walked through my apartment door, and I left Rebecca and the beagle in the living room while I paced around my bedroom, trying to think of what to do next. After a quick online search, I found that Pine Brook didn't have any women's shelters, and the nearest one was a thirty-minute drive.

This seemed bigger than just taking Rebecca to a shelter, though. Given the violence David had shown to Rebecca and to me, plus the truck that had run me off the road, I had a strong suspicion that he had killed his mother-in-law. I needed to involve the police in this if we were going to find the truth.

Finally, I called Miriam. She'd given me her cell phone number a few months back, as she'd wanted to share a chocolate chip cookie recipe with me. I'd never made the recipe, but I'd made sure to save her number in case I needed it for something just like this.

"Miriam? It's Simone. I'm sorry for calling so late, but I need your help. I'm trying to get ahold of Detective Patel, but she's not answering my calls. Do you happen to have a number for Officer Scott? It's an emergency."

"Of course, dear," Miriam said, her voice surprised. She rattled off a number, which I quickly wrote down on a scrap of paper. "Is there anything I can help you with?" she asked.

"No, but you might end up with a lot of paperwork in the morning. Thanks for your help." We said our goodbyes and hung up, then I quickly dialed Officer Scott.

He and I weren't exactly friends, and on more than one occasion, he'd told me to stay out of police business. However, I knew he'd handle something like this the right way, unlike some of the other cops down at the station. I had to hope that he had another way of getting in touch with Patel.

"Officer Scott, it's Simone Evans. I apologize for calling so late, but I'm trying to get in touch with Detective Patel. I have some information regarding the death of Kathleen Richards, and a potential abuse situation. Can you help me?"

An hour later, Rebecca and I sat in a conference room at the police station. Rebecca was a tense ball of nerves, sitting completely still and rigid in her seat. I shifted around in my chair, trying to find a comfortable position but failing in these plastic monstrosities the police called chairs. After a moment, the conference room door opened and Patel entered. I stopped my squirming and leaned forward in my seat.

"We picked up your husband at your house," she said to Rebecca, taking a seat across from the two of us with a file in her hand. "He initially denied your claims, but he ended up getting aggressive and shoved one of my officers, so we arrested him for that. He broke down on the drive over and admitted to the abuse. I guess he couldn't keep it inside any longer. He's in one of the back rooms right now, writing a statement."

Rebecca let out a *whoosh* of air, all her adrenaline from the night leaving her body in one fell swoop. She braced her hands against the table, steadying herself, and I rubbed her back soothingly.

"What's going to happen now?" I asked after a moment, when it was clear Rebecca wasn't going to say anything.

Patel's eyes darted to me, unreadable. "Assuming Mrs. Lewis would like to press charges, I'll need to take her statement and send it off to the county D.A. We'll hold your husband here tonight while we get all the details worked out, then tomorrow someone from Victim's Services will come by your house to help you create a plan for next steps."

Rebecca didn't speak for a moment, then nodded her head vigorously, her gaze steely. "I'd like to press charges. What do I need to do?"

A smile crept across Patel's face at her words., grateful that Rebecca was going to hold her husband accountable for what he'd done. Patel cleared her throat and straightened up in her seat, hiding the smile quickly, and passed the file in her hand across to Rebecca. "There's paper and a pen in there. Right down everything you can remember—all the times he hurt you, all the times he threatened you. Take as long as you need." She stood up, turning to me. "Simone, may I speak with you for a moment?"

I squeezed Rebecca's arm encouragingly and followed Patel out of the room, the sound of Rebecca's frantic writing on the paper drifting out after us.

Patel led me away from the conference room and down a short hallway, stopping once we were away from any prying ears. She crossed her arms and narrowed her eyes at me. "What exactly happened tonight?" she asked, her voice low.

"I went by the mechanic's shop and ran into Rebecca. She, um, broke down and told me about David's abuse. I tried calling you but you weren't answering, so I reached out to Officer Scott, instead. I guess he has another way of getting ahold of you." How likely would it be that Patel would give me that number, too? Not likely.

"What's this I hear about you almost getting run over by a truck earlier today?"

Jeez, I'd almost forgotten all about that in the chaos of the evening. "Right. Um, that's why I'd gone to the mechanic's shop. I thought I'd seen the truck that was used in the shop, and I thought maybe David was the one who came after me."

"Why didn't you tell the police about the truck, instead of sneaking around to find it yourself?"

"I did tell the police! Well, I told Officer Collins I couldn't really tell what it looked like beyond the color, and I wasn't certain that I'd seen the same one at the mechanic's shop. I didn't want to go back without more proof, so I figured I'd look around the shop through the windows and see if I could find it." Since I hadn't actually broken into the mechanic's shop, what I'd done wasn't exactly illegal, but sometimes Detective Patel and I had different definitions of what was and wasn't legal.

"I'm assuming Rebecca caught you sneaking around. And she just immediately shared about what her husband had done to her?"

I hesitated, then nodded. Patel probably wouldn't appreciate it if she knew that I'd basically accused Rebecca of murder, and that was what had gotten her to open up to me.

"I'm sure he killed Kathleen, too. He wanted her house, so maybe he got upset with her one day and pushed her down the stairs. He's a really violent guy. I'm sure Rebecca will put that in her statement, too. Then you can bring him up on murder charges."

Patel sighed deeply and studied me, clearly disappointed in me for sticking my nose into a police investigation again. "Let's go check on Rebecca," she said finally, turning around and striding back towards the conference room.

That was it? She wasn't going to berate me for getting involved in her murder investigation again? Maybe saving someone from an abusive marriage got me off the hook.

Back in the room, Rebecca slid the file folder back to Patel. "It's all in there."

Patel picked up her statement and flipped through the pages, her brow furrowing as she skimmed the words. "I don't see anything about your mother. I thought you said he killed Kathleen?" she directed to me.

"No, he didn't," Rebecca said, sitting up in her chair. "He might've done a lot of bad things to me, but he's not a killer."

"Are you sure?" I asked her, sitting down across from her. "How can you be so positive?"

"Because I was with him the night she was killed. He... he hit me, then he got drunk and passed out in front of the TV. I stayed up all night, waiting for him to wake up and come after me again, but he was out for the whole night. There was no way he could've left without me hearing him."

I sat back in my seat, processing her words. I'd been so certain that David had come after me with the truck and had killed Kathleen, but if what Rebecca said was true...

"Where was he today, in the afternoon?" I asked, needing confirmation about the truck.

"He had a job out in Tacoma all day."

"What was he driving when he left?"

Rebecca frowned, then thought for a moment. "A white SUV. He had to take a bunch of parts with him, so he needed the extra space in the back. Why?"

The truck I saw definitely wasn't white. "What about that black truck in the garage? I saw it earlier. Could he have used that to attack me?"

Rebecca shook her head. "That truck's engine has been broken for weeks. That's why it's in our garage. David's trying to fix it."

I sat back in my seat, stunned. That truck didn't work, and David had been out of town today in a white truck. He wasn't the one who attacked me?

"If you're finished," Patel said, casting a stern gaze my way for getting in the middle of her interview, "I'd like to have you sign this. Then you're free to leave."

"Simone, will you stay with me?" Rebecca asked, reaching out and grabbing my hands. "I-I don't want to be alone right now."

I smiled and squeezed her hands in return. "Of course. I'll be here when you're ready to leave."

Twenty minutes later, Rebecca had finished signing what she needed to sign, and I drove us out of the police station parking lot. "Back to your house?" I asked, turning up the heat in the car.

She shook her head. "I can't go back there. What if he comes home?"

"You heard Detective Patel. He's not leaving that station until he's arraigned by a judge, and that won't be at least until tomorrow morning. And even once he's arraigned, the D.A. should immediately file charges against him, and he'll have to wait until his bail hearing before he has even a chance of leaving police custody. Once we get you in touch with a lawyer, you can file a restraining order and take full control of your house. You're safe now."

"I don't feel very safe." She wrapped her arms around herself, her hands shaking. "Can I come back with you? I'll feel safer knowing you're close by, after everything you've done for me."

I nodded. "Of course. You'll have to sleep on the couch, and a certain beagle might decide to sleep with you. But you're always welcome."

"Thank you. And thank you for looking into my mother's death. I know I was rude to you at her funeral, but I didn't want to even consider that someone had actually killed her. It was too much to handle with everything else going on."

"I completely understand. I'm sure all of this has been so hard for you, but at least you're safe now. If David didn't kill your mother, can you think of any reason why someone would want to hurt her?"

"I'm not sure. She was such a kind woman to everyone

she met. Well, except for her neighbor, Joseph, but I suppose there's no way he could've done it, right, now that he's dead? Not unless there are two killers out there."

My hands tightened on the steering wheel. Man, I sure hoped not, or else that was going to make finding the killer much harder.

"She used to keep a lot of money in the house when I was younger," Rebecca continued. "She never trusted banks. Maybe someone learned about that."

"Did she still keep money in her house?"

"I'm not sure. As you know, we weren't very close these last few years. She never left anything lying around, but she'd find ways to hide it in the walls or other secret places. I remember, as a teenager, asking for some cash to go to the movies, and she pulled a twenty dollar bill right out of the wall in the kitchen. It was the strangest thing I'd ever seen, but that's the kind of person my mother was."

Did Paula know about the money in the house? She'd been spending a lot of time there since Kathleen had passed away, claiming to be helping pack things up, but was she really looking for this money? Would Kathleen have told her about it?

I yawned, a wave of exhaustion hitting me. I wasn't going to get any answers tonight, not this late, but it was something to look into tomorrow. Right now, I needed to get Rebecca back to my house safely.

Lola was snoring on the couch when we got home, but she quickly woke up and greeted Rebecca with kisses when she heard us arrive. I found an extra blanket and pillow for Rebecca and got her set up on the couch.

"No Christmas tree?" she asked, looking around my bare living room.

I grimaced. "I've been busy. It's a long story."

She smiled. "It's okay, I understand. This town is so obsessed with Christmas, it's surprising to go anywhere and not see a tree."

She was right, Pine Brook was obsessed with Christmas, but a part of me really liked it. Though it did mean I still had a bunch of Christmas cards I needed to send out.

"I wanted to ask you about something weird I heard about your mother," I said as Rebecca settled herself on the couch. "Joseph told me he could hear singing coming from Kathleen's house at all hours. Do you know anything about that?"

"Oh, yes, my mother loved singing. She'd been into it ever since I was a kid. I always thought it was embarrassing when I was younger—what teenager wants their mother going around, singing everywhere?—but it was really rather sweet. She had a great singing voice."

Once she said it like that, I realized it was silly of me to assume that singing could be anything suspicious. Joseph's own dislike of Kathleen had caused him to think something strange was going on because of the singing, and my determination to find her killer had led me to believe that the singing was strange, too. When, really, she was just an old woman trying to keep herself company, all alone in her big house.

"You know," Rebecca said, seated on the couch and petting Lola, staring off into the distance, "part of me wonders if all of this would've happened if my mom and I hadn't drifted apart. If I'd been more willing to talk to her about what was going on in my life, and not let the distance grow between us." She looked up at me then, tears shining in her eyes. "Your mother is in town, isn't she? Someone mentioned that to me. You should appreciate your relationship with her while you still can." At that, she curled up on the couch and pulled the blanket over her head, slowly drifting to sleep.

I turned off the light and padded into my bedroom, another yawn overtaking me. I was still determined to find Kathleen's killer, but maybe Rebecca was right and I should focus more on healing my own relationships right now.

18

The next morning, I left Rebecca in my apartment with Lola by her side. She'd gotten a call from Victim's Services, and someone was going to stop by to help her start the process of finding a lawyer, initiating her divorce, and figuring out how she could keep her house and her business while her husband went to jail. Rebecca wasn't interested in running the mechanic's shop on her own, but if she could sell it and Kathleen's house, then she'd have a nice nest egg for herself as she figured out what she wanted to do with the rest of her life.

Snowflakes fell from the sky as I slowly drove to the inn, the winter storm that had been in the forecast all week finally here. When I'd woken up, I'd sent Patel a text message letting her know that Kathleen had kept money in her house, and that I suspected Paula might've known about the money. Patel had a lot of things on her plate right now, so I wasn't sure if she'd follow up on this lead without much evidence, but I didn't want to keep this information to myself. Right now, though, I had a relationship to repair.

Once at the inn, I hung up my coat and warmed my

hands by the fire, preparing myself to go talk to my mom. I didn't want to let things get worse between us, like they had with Kathleen and Rebecca. If she didn't want to talk about Sylvia's letter, I was okay with that, but I wanted to make sure she knew how much I appreciated her.

"Simone!" Estelle and Miles entered the lobby at that moment, hurrying over to my side.

"Hey, you two. What's going on?" I glanced up at the staircase. Maybe I wasn't totally ready to go talk to my mom just yet, and I could use these two as a distraction while I worked up the courage.

"Estelle has something she'd like to say," Miles said, gesturing to his wife.

"I'm sorry for acting so crazy with Kathleen's death," she said. "I guess I've been a little freaked out now that she's gone, especially since I'm almost her age. I didn't want to think about my potential death, so I got it in my head that someone had killed her."

"Well, I mean, you were right about that part."

Estelle waved her hand flippantly. "Sure, and I do hope we find her killer. But I think I was covering up my true feelings by diving into this investigation, and I should've been more careful. I'm going to try to take things more slowly from now on."

I glanced over at Miles, who was smiling as he stared at his wife. Guess he was right about her being afraid of her mortality. I was glad to hear that Estelle was going to try to be careful from now on, though I hoped she wouldn't lose her quintessential spunk.

"Miles, how is your hip?" I asked. "I'm glad to see you moving around, but I just hope you aren't pushing yourself too far."

Miles smiled gently. "I appreciate your concern. It's

doing a lot better, and my doctor said I can go back to my regular routine."

"A routine that mostly consists of feeding Lola treats and playing chess in the park," Estelle added jokingly, her eyes twinkling.

Miles grinned at his wife and tapped his temple with two fingers. "Gotta keep the old noggin active."

Estelle patted his hand. "It's scary getting old, don't get me wrong," she went on, turning back to me. "But I'm so happy I get to spend these years with this guy, even if he still won't play chess with me."

"Hey, I've tried to teach you! It's a game that requires patience, which you are sometimes lacking in."

"Yeah, patience and an affinity for dullness," Estelle quipped, shooting me a wink.

I smiled as I watched these two quibble. They'd been married for so long, and the spark was still so strong between them. It was hard to imagine attaching yourself to another person for the rest of your life, but watching this couple, I could see the benefits of committing to a partner who loved and cared for you as strongly as they did.

Nick's face flashed across my mind. I loved him, I really did, and I could see us growing old together, just like Estelle and Miles. I wanted him to be the person I stared across the table at when my hips got sore and I spent more time resting and reminiscing about the past.

Wow, where had that thought come from? I'd only been considering moving in with Nick the past few days, but once I really thought about it... I realized I wanted more from him. I just hoped he felt the same about me.

I had time to talk to Nick about the future of our relationship, and I wasn't going to run away from that conversation. For now, though, I wanted to update Estelle on the case. She had been right to be worried about Kathleen, now that we knew there was a killer out there, and I wanted to do what I could to help her move on from Kathleen's death by finding the culprit.

"There has actually been a development in the case," I said, settling us down on the couches in the lobby. I explained about the attack from the truck the day before, snooping around the mechanic's shop and getting caught by Rebecca, then learning about her abusive marriage to David.

"Rebecca said she was with David the night her mother was killed, so she doesn't think he did it. But he's going to get into a lot of trouble for what he's done to Rebecca."

"Oh, dear." Estelle sat back in her seat, her eyes sad. "That must've been so tough for her to admit. And I'm sure Kathleen was heartbroken that she couldn't do anything to save her daughter. I'm glad Rebecca is getting the help she needs now."

"Me too. There's one other thing." I quickly explained what Rebecca had told me about her mom hiding money in her house. "Did you know about this?" I asked Estelle.

"No, but I'm not surprised. Kathleen did always seem weird about banks, and I can't actually remember her ever going into one. Do you think there's still money in her house?"

"I'm not sure. I told Detective Patel about it, so hopefully she'll investigate. I think it's best if I stay out of things for now. Actually, there's one other thing I need to take care of. My mom and I got into a fight, and I want to apologize to her. After learning about Rebecca's relationship with Kathleen, I don't want that to happen between us. I'm just scared to talk to her."

"Why are you scared?" Estelle asked.

I let out a sigh. "I don't know. I'm just worried about disappointing her. I've not always done a good job of living up to her standards, and I don't want her to be ashamed of me anymore."

Miles grabbed my hand in his. "There's no way she could be ashamed of you, because you're an amazing woman. Anyone would be proud to have you as their daughter."

Tears pricked at my eyes at his words. "Thank you," I said, squeezing his hand.

Estelle glanced at her watch. "We better get going," she said, standing up and pulling Miles up with her. "We're helping with the toy drive downtown, and we can't be late for our shift." They both waved goodbye, then dashed out of the inn, as sprightly as ever.

I smiled as I watched them leave, then went to the front desk to check on any business. The lobby was quiet, Tracy off somewhere else, and I let my mind settle as I flipped through the mail, the sound of the crackling fireplace filling the space.

I groaned as I came upon another Christmas card from someone in town. Jeez, I still hadn't gotten around to sending out cards, and Christmas was quickly approaching. Why couldn't I handle even one simple task like this?

"No, stop beating yourself up," I murmured to myself, shaking off my glumness about these cards and pulling out a pad of paper and a pen. I still had time, and I'd get these done today. I began making a list down the page, resting my elbows on the desk as I wrote.

Twenty minutes later, I had a list longer than my arm and a plan for getting cards in the mail by the end of the week. Maybe a couple would arrive after the new year, but that wasn't so bad, was it? What mattered was the thought I was putting into sending a nice message to my loved ones.

"Uhh, Simone? I'm going to need your help in here." Eddy came out of the bistro, holding a pile of wet washcloths. Uh-oh, what had happened back there?

"Excuse me." A guest approached the front desk, wrapped in a robe from the spa. "I've got an appointment for a massage, but there's no one back there to massage me!"

"Christmas wreath delivery for Tracy Williams. Where should I put them?" A deliveryman entered the lobby through the back, his arms full of ginormous wreaths. Why did Tracy order us more wreaths? The Hemlock was already bursting with Christmas decorations.

"Simone?" Eddy shifted his weight between his feet, his eyes wide and nervous as he gripped the wet towels.

"Hello?" the guest asked, as if I hadn't seen her standing right in front of me. "Is someone going to give me a massage or what?"

"These are getting kind of heavy," the deliveryman said as pine needles began falling off the wreaths. "Maybe I should set them down here?" He pointed to one of the couches where another guest sat, who shrunk away as the man came closer with a ridiculous number of wreaths.

Oh, goodness, where was Tracy when I needed her? This was why Nadia couldn't go on two-month-long cruises; no matter how smoothly things seemed to be running at the inn, there was always another catastrophe to deal with, and I couldn't handle all of this alone.

Except...maybe I could. I mean, I had to now. I didn't have any choice. None of these people were going away, and I couldn't have wet towels dripping in the lobby, Christmas wreaths strewn all about, and angry guests demanding a massage. There was no one here to help me, which meant I only had one option.

"Eddy, I don't know what's happening back there, but there are extra towels in the pantry in the kitchen, and Javier should know how to turn off the water supply in the kitchen before it all starts flooding. Sir." I turned to the deliveryman and pointed to an empty bin behind the front desk. "You can put those right here. Send us a bill later. And ma'am, I'm so sorry for the delay," I added, focusing my attention on the robed guest. "What's your last name? I'll look up your reservation and find out where your massage therapist is."

Slowly, the chaos in the lobby settled down, as Eddy left to deal with the mess in the bistro with the help of Javier and Penny, the Christmas wreaths were signed over to me, and I discovered that the guest had arrived too early for her massage. I added a free facial to her appointment to keep her happy, and sent everyone off with their problems solved.

Once alone, I stretched my back and let out a sigh. Maybe I was actually perfectly capable of running the inn on my own... I couldn't do it completely on my own, of course, but maybe it wasn't so bad if Nadia or Tracy took a vacation every once in a while.

"Wow, that was impressive." My mom appeared in the lobby, her smile bright. "I thought we were efficient at my clinic since we deal with sick people, but you managed to handle all of that much better than I've ever run a business. What a great job."

My dark cheeks warmed at her compliment, and I straightened up behind the desk. "I didn't think anyone saw that. But thank you. I'm starting to realize I'm pretty good at this, too."

"I always knew you would do great things, but seeing

how wonderfully you handled all those issues... You should be proud of yourself. I know I am."

Tension eased from my shoulders at her words. I'd been so anxious about her visit when she first showed up, wanting to impress her and showing her that I could live up to her high standards. But she'd been nothing but kind about my business since she arrived, and I'd seen the pride etched across her face for days. Was I actually the one holding myself to these high standards, and not my mother? Could I find a way to treat myself more kindly and remind myself that I was capable of running a successful business?

"Can we talk?" my mom asked, motioning to one of the empty couches. I nodded and came to sit next to her.

"I'm so sorry about my outburst yesterday," she said once we were seated. "It wasn't fair to you, and I shouldn't have said what I said."

"I'm sorry for pestering you with all those questions about Aunt Sylvia. It's your story to tell, and I shouldn't have tried to make you do something you didn't want to."

"No, you have a right to know. I mean, you're running Sylvia's inn, for goodness sake. How could I not tell you what really happened between us? I've just regretted not working things out with her sooner. And I'm ashamed that you two didn't have a closer relationship before she died. She was a great woman, and you deserved to know her as an adult."

"I do feel like I've gotten to know her now that I'm running this inn and through learning about her from everyone in Pine Brook. They all have such great things to say."

"I'm glad to hear that." My mom smiled and looked down at the couch between us. "Sylvia and I used to be much closer when we were younger. Similar to how you and

Chrissy are. As you know, Sylvia was older than me, and I always looked up to her. When our parents passed away, back when you were in college, Sylvia had a hard time dealing with it. She was also struggling with her sexuality and her marriage to Tim, and she just started pulling away from me."

So my mom had known that Sylvia was bisexual. She'd never said as much to me before, but it made sense that Sylvia would've told her sister since they were so close when they were younger. Maybe Tracy shouldn't have been so afraid to talk to my mom about her relationship with Sylvia.

"She wouldn't be honest with me about what was going on in her life," she went on, "and there was suddenly a wedge between us. I tried to bridge the gap, but it became too hard, and I started to get mad at her because it felt like she wasn't trying. I never really considered what she was going through during that time. One year passed, then two, and suddenly it was ten years later, and I didn't know how to talk to her again, even if I wanted to. We just let all these words go unspoken, and our relationship was never the same. She thought I judged her for who she was, when really I was upset that she wouldn't talk to me about what was going on in her life anymore. The more she pulled away, the more upset I got, and something was broken between us. I didn't know how to repair it, and it became easier to simply ignore it."

I grabbed a tissue from one of the side tables and passed it to my mom, dabbing at my own eyes with a tissue as she spoke. I'd had no idea things had gotten so bad between them. We'd spent less time with Sylvia as we'd gotten older, but I never knew that this was why.

She took in a deep breath and let out a slow exhale, smiling weakly. "Sylvia wrote me a letter, too, before she passed away. She apologized for letting our estrangement go on for so long, and she said she wished that we'd had more time together. She said she hoped I could learn to love this inn like she had, and even though I've only been here for a week, I really think I'm starting to. You've done an amazing job of continuing Sylvia's legacy here."

I smiled and pulled her into a hug, squeezing her tight. "Thank you. That means the world to me. I-I've been really self-conscious ever since you got here. I haven't been able to keep a job in years, and I was worried you'd be disappointed in me."

"Oh, honey, but I'm so proud of you! And I always have been. Look at the way you handled all those people just now. You never have to worry about that with me. You're such an amazing person."

"It's not just that, though. Tracy has been such a great business partner to me, and now that she's thinking about going on this long trip…I'm worried I won't be able to run this place without her."

My mom reached out and held my hands between hers. "Do you remember when you were six, and you decided you were going to raise money to save the elephants in Africa?"

I let out a bark of laughter. "Wow, I haven't thought about that in years. Why did I think I could do that?"

"You've always been a very determined little girl. You marched up to me and your father and declared what you were going to do, then you roped in your sister and began selling lemonade on the corner. When you ran out of lemons, then you started making friendship bracelets and sold those to kids at school. When your teacher said you couldn't sell things during school hours, you started collecting empty soda bottles and sending them in to get recycled and collected pennies for them. And not once did you ask for any help with this. Your father and I tried, of course, and we made sure to drive you to the recycling plant so you didn't have to get there on your own. By the end of that year, you'd raised almost a thousand dollars, and you found a non-profit in Kenya to send the money to."

"Oh man, I had no idea I was such a precocious child," I said with a laugh. "I'm sure I was a nightmare to deal with."

She rolled her eyes and chuckled. "The point of that story is that you've always been able to accomplish anything you set your mind to. You've maybe been adrift over the years, floating to different jobs, but you're doing an excellent job here, and I know you'll do amazing even if Tracy is gone for a little while. Six months will be over before you know it."

My face warmed up at her words. Maybe she was right and I would be able to handle this. I had a great team at the inn, and I was determined to do what I could to make sure the Hemlock stayed successful. Nadia would be back soon, and even if she decided to spend the rest of her days relaxing on a Greek beach with Christos, I'd still be able to find a way to keep the Hemlock successful.

My mother swiped at the last tears on her face, straightening up in her seat. "All right, enough about all of that. What's happening with Kathleen's murder? Have you found the killer?"

I smiled. Of course she'd bring it back to the investigation. She was my mother, after all, and she'd always encouraged Chrissy's true crime obsession.

"Actually, a lot has happened with that." I explained everything that had happened in the past twenty-four hours, from the truck attack, to snooping on Rebecca and learning about her abusive husband, and what she'd told me about the money in Kathleen's house.

"I told Detective Patel about the money, but she hasn't called me back yet. I don't know if she's gone looking for it yet."

"Why don't we try to find it? We can go later tonight, once it's dark, and we'll make sure the house is empty before going inside. If we can find proof that Paula has been looking for this money, too, then we can bring that to the police."

"I don't know," I said slowly, concern and a little bit of excitement coursing through me at the thought of finally finding Kathleen's killer. "I don't think we should go breaking into Kathleen's house."

"Go ask Rebecca for a key, then. That way, it won't be a crime."

Her logic wasn't exactly airtight, but I was eager to get to the bottom of Kathleen's death. "Hmm. Alright. If I don't hear back from Patel by the end of the day, then we'll go do some snooping."

"Yippee!" My mom clapped her hands together in joy, and I held back a groan. How much was I going to regret this plan later?

19

Nightfall came quickly. Still no word from Detective Patel. I'd managed to get in touch with Rebecca and asked her about a key to Kathleen's house. She was still with Victim's Services, making a plan for how to leave her abusive husband and make sure he never had another chance to hurt someone else, so she wasn't able to meet up with me and give me a key to her mother's home. However, she said that Kathleen had always left a spare key under a rock in her garden, and I could get into her house that way. I didn't want to get caught sneaking around Kathleen's backyard at night, looking for the spare key, so I'd left the inn briefly during lunch to pick up the key in case we needed it.

When I'd spoken with Rebecca, she was hesitant about letting me into her mother's house. "Are you sure this is a good idea? I mean, I barely know you. Where are you even going to start looking?"

"I know this is a big request," I'd told her, my voice pleading. "But I'm just trying to do right by your mother. If there's proof in her house about what happened to her, I need to find it."

She let out a sigh, not speaking for a moment. "It might be useful for me to have that money," she said finally. "This divorce is going to be expensive, and my assets will be tied up for a while as I deal with the fallout from what David did. I could really use that money, and I want to find my mom's killer as much as you."

"Thank you. I promise I'll be careful. Do you know what time Paula normally leaves your mom's house?" I didn't want to sneak in while Paula was still around.

"Oh, she told me she wouldn't be able to pack stuff for a couple days because she has a job interview in Seattle. She shouldn't be there."

"That's good to know." If Paula was the killer, I didn't want her to catch me looking for evidence of her guilt. "I'll call you as soon as I learn anything."

Now that the time was approaching to get into Kathleen's house and search for evidence that Paula was trying to find Kathleen's money, I was starting to have second thoughts about this entire plan. Yes, we had permission from Rebecca to look around, but I didn't know what we were going to find, and after the truck attack, I wasn't eager to put myself back in the crosshairs of a killer.

My mom, however, had a different feeling about the whole matter.

"Come on, it'll be fine," she said that night, once the lobby had cleared and the bistro had shut down for the night. "We'll be perfectly safe. We just need to look around and see what we can find."

I sighed. With Paula out of town, this might've been our best opportunity to get proof for the police. Detective Patel still hadn't called me back, so I had no idea if she was gathering evidence against Paula. If we could find something in Kathleen's house, we could hopefully help the police arrest the killer. And, if there wasn't anything to find there, and Patel learned about what we'd done, we could say that Rebecca had given us permission to look around her mother's home. I didn't know exactly what we'd find, but I had a sense that the truth was somewhere inside.

"Fine, let's do it," I said. "But we're going to be careful about this, understand? We don't know for sure who the killer is, and we don't want Kathleen's neighbors calling the police because they see us sneaking around. Let's keep the lights off and be quick about this, okay?"

"Excellent, let's go!" My mom gathered up her things and dashed out of the inn, and I followed after her more slowly, shaking my head as I went. This was not a great plan, but we were running out of options to find Kathleen's killer.

We drove across town, my mom bouncing in the passenger seat with excitement as we went. Kathleen's street was quiet as we approached, no lights on in Kathleen's house or Cassie's house. It was almost nine o'clock at night, so maybe the neighbor had already gone to bed for the night. Hopefully she wouldn't show up and get concerned about a car parked in front of Kathleen's house.

The key I'd picked up earlier in the day turned easily in Kathleen's door, and we quickly snuck into the house. I shut the door behind us gently, then turned and took stock of the living room. Boxes were stacked up around the place—looked like Paula was making progress packing up Kathleen's house for Rebecca. Was she doing anything else here that she shouldn't?

A curse came from deeper in the house, and we paused at the front door.

"Someone's here," my mom whispered, taking a step further into the house.

I held out a hand to stop her. "We should leave," I hissed back. "Whoever is here probably doesn't want to be found, if they're keeping all the lights off. Let's call the police."

"We need proof, okay? They could leave before the police get here. Let's just take a little look." Before I could stop her, my mom tiptoed through the living room towards the back of Kathleen's house.

I held back a groan, hurrying after her. Why did I keep hanging out with women who just wanted to rush into danger all the time?

There was a small sitting room in the back of Kathleen's house, and I paused on the threshold of the room next to my mom. My eyes needed a second to process what they were seeing.

Paula stood at the wall with a hammer in hand, digging into a hole she'd created in the wall. She swore again, her frustration clear from this far away.

My mom let out a gasp of the sight of Paula, and the nurse spun around once she realized she wasn't alone, her eyes wide. A gun was tucked into her waistband, and my mouth went dry at the sight.

"Sorry, we were just, uh, leaving," I said, grabbing my mother's arm and stumbling backwards out of the room.

Paula dropped the hammer and pulled the gun out of her waistband, aiming it at us. Her hand shook as she held it. "Stay there. Nobody move. What do you think you're doing?"

"I-I thought you were out of town," I stammered, my brain spinning a mile a minute as I tried to process what was happening. "Rebecca said you had a job interview."

"I just told her that so that no one would come looking for me."

"Paula, I don't know what you think is going on here," my mom said, leaning forward, "but we just came by to pick something up for Rebecca. Sh-she finally left her husband, and she's been busy with paperwork all day. She asked us to pick up a photo album for her. She's been grieving her mother's death and just wanted something to comfort her while she's going through her divorce."

My eyebrows rose. As far as lies went, that wasn't too bad. Unfortunately, Paula didn't seem convinced.

"Does anyone know you're here?" she asked.

I shook my head slowly, trying to come up with a plan. "No one has to know. W-we can leave you to whatever it is you're doing, and be on our way."

"There's no need to have a gun out," my mom added. "We just came for the photo album, and we can get out of your hair. No one has to know what happened here."

Paula let out a deep exhale, rubbing the side of her face with her free hand. "I think it's too late for that now. I don't have much time, and I need to find that money. Both of you, in the living room."

We backed out of the room and followed her instructions, exiting the kitchen and walking into the living room. She went into the coat closet near the front door and pulled out some rope, tossing it to us.

"You, tie her up," she said to my mom, pointing at my wrists.

Once my hands were bound, Paula put her gun back in her waistband and tied up my mom's wrists, then made us sit back on the couch. She quickly tied up our ankles as well, then began pacing in front of us, chewing on one of her nails.

"I don't understand," I said once we were tied up. "Why are you doing this?"

Paula furrowed her brow and began walking around the living room, looking into baskets and checking the closet. "I ran out of time. I've spent the past week searching this house, top to bottom, looking for that money, but I can't find it. Then, the police were at my apartment earlier today. Can you believe that? Fortunately, I saw them before I went home, but it's clear now that I don't have enough time to keep looking. I came back here tonight to check this place out one more time, but I think I'm going to have to give up."

"But I don't understand—what money are you talking about?" I asked. My mom glanced over at me, probably wondering why I was lying, but I didn't react. This wasn't the first time I'd faced down a killer with a gun. If I could keep Paula talking, it might give us enough time to come up with a plan to escape. Though, with our hands bound up like this, I had no idea how we were going to get out of this one.

Paula sighed and came to stand before us, her hands on her hips. "I may as well tell you. You're going to die tonight, anyway. Maybe you know where the money is. Kathleen, in all her wonderful glory, never trusted banks. That's sometimes common with older folks. Instead, she kept her money somewhere in her house. That's what I've been looking for since she died, but I can't find it. I'm starting to think the old woman was lying to me when she said that."

"So Kathleen tells you she keeps money in her house, and then she fell and died, giving you a perfect chance to snoop around and look for the money?" I asked.

"Oh, it didn't go quite like that," Paula said. "I expected her to die on her own pretty quickly. I only take on clients in their seventies since their life expectancy is pretty short at that age. But Kathleen was spunkier than I expected. I could easily see her living until her nineties. Once she told me about the money, and that her daughter was trying to get her into a nursing home, I had to act fast. I couldn't let Rebecca take over this house and find the money herself."

"So you killed her?" my mom asked, incredulity in her voice. "All for this money?"

"And I can't even find it now," Paula said with a shrug. "Such a waste." She sighed and ran a hand through her hair, her hands still shaking. "Everything's gotten out of control. I'm not a murderer, I swear, but I need to find that money... If Kathleen had just told me where it was, none of this would've happened."

"That's why Kathleen's house was so messy before," I said as realization dawned, unable to keep myself from talking. "She found you looking for the money, didn't she?"

Paula nodded, letting out a sigh. "I thought I was being quiet, but this house is so big, and everything creaks all the time. Kathleen had just gone down for bed, but she came out when she heard me moving around. I tried to reason with her, tried to explain away what I was doing, but she wouldn't listen. She went to the stairs to get to her landline downstairs to call the police, and I couldn't let her go. I...I grabbed her. I was just trying to hold her back, wrapping my arms around her shoulders, but then I was gripping her neck, and everything was moving so fast...I held her too tight, and she slipped on the hardwood floor, and then suddenly she was lying at the bottom of the stairs." She fell silent as she admitted what she'd done, hanging her head and breathing deeply at her admission. "It was just an accident," she muttered, either trying to convince herself or convince us, I wasn't quite sure.

"What happened with Joseph?" I asked. "That definitely wasn't an accident."

A cloud passed over Paula's face. "I didn't want to do that, but I caught him looking through the window with a pair of binoculars while I was tearing into the drywall upstairs. He always was too nosy about what went on in this house. Very suspicious man. I couldn't risk him telling the police about what he'd seen, so the next day I snuck into his house and put peanut oil in his coffee grounds. I'd seen him sitting out on his porch with coffee every morning, so I knew he'd drink it and that would be the end of him."

My mom gasped at that. "You're a monster!"

Paula spun around and trained the gun back on us. "I do what I have to do to survive. I never wanted to kill anyone, but I need that money."

A chill raced down my spine at her callousness. "It was you that came after me in that truck, wasn't it? But you don't drive a truck."

She nodded, her face stony. "Sorry about that, but you were getting too close to the truth. I needed to get you out of the way. Who knew it's actually pretty tough to run someone down with a truck? I had to steal it because I couldn't use my own car and have it traced back to me. All that effort, and it didn't even work. You wouldn't stay away. But I'm not going to let myself get caught, not after all this time. Shut up while I think."

"What's your plan here?" I asked, unable to stop myself. She was nervous, I could tell, and even though she had killed two people and tried to kill me, maybe there was a way to talk her out of shooting us, too. "Like you said, you've run out of time. If you haven't found the money yet, you aren't going to find it now. And the police are looking for you."

"Yes, it's true that I'm in a bit of a pickle, but fortunately this isn't my first time cleaning up one of my messes. I'm not happy that I now have to deal with the two of you, but I'll just shoot you both and then leave town. I'm an expert at creating a new life for myself, but I have to try to find that money if I can." With that, she stormed out of the living room and went back to the sitting room we'd just come from.

My mom whimpered as tears began falling down her face. "Simone, what are we going to do?" she whispered.

"It's okay, I'll get us out of this," I said, beginning to work my wrists together to try to loosen the rope. Unfortunately for me, my mom was apparently very good at tying rope, as there wasn't any give in the rope. "Can you get that off?" I asked, gesturing to her rope. Maybe if she could slip out of her binds, she could untie me and we could get out of here before Paula came back.

"Simone, look at me."

I glanced up, surprised at her tone. Her gaze was steely and determined. "Simone, I'm so proud of you and everything you have accomplished. I love you so much, and if I have to die like this, I'm glad it's with you."

"Mom, don't say that! We can get out of this." I doubled my efforts to loosen the rope around my wrists, but it wasn't looking good. I needed a knife or something else sharp. Were we about to die? Tears began pouring down my face as the reality of the situation came over me.

Just then, a crash came from the back of the house, followed by a whimper. Suddenly, Estelle appeared in the living room and hurried over to us, quickly releasing us from our bound wrists.

"Estelle, what are you doing here?" I asked, shock in my voice.

"Saving you, of course," she said with a wink. "I hit Paula

over the head with a frying pan, and I called the police. We're safe."

The three of us hugged, adrenaline coursing through my veins. After all that, and Estelle had saved the day.

20

"So Paula was just after Kathleen's money? And she'd done this before?" Miles asked.

I nodded and took a sip of my hot chocolate. "Apparently, she's run this scam throughout the U.S. over the years, but this is the first time it's ever led to murder. Detective Patel said there are a bunch of other district attorneys across the country who want their chance to try Paula for what she did in their states, too."

It was the next morning, and I was back at the bistro, nursing a cup of hot chocolate while I was questioned by various townsfolk about what had happened the night before. Once Estelle had shown up and saved the day, we'd called the police and explained everything that had happened.

Detective Patel had arrived on scene, explaining that she'd spent the day in Holliston, where she'd been looking into another suspicious eldercare scam that she could tie back to Paula. That's why she hadn't been around when I'd tried calling her all day, but once she learned about what happened at Kathleen's house, she was quick to get our statements and add it as evidence to the case she was building against Paula.

"It's so sad that Kathleen had to die, but I'm glad Paula has been caught," Eddy said, leaning against the back of Miles' chair. "At least now she won't be able to hurt anyone else."

"Where do you think all the money is?" Miles asked.

I shrugged. "Probably in the walls. That would explain why Paula had started digging into them. She'd searched through all the obvious places, but couldn't find it. Kathleen was smart enough to get creative about where she hid it so that no one would find it easily. Hopefully Rebecca can find the money and do something good with it."

The police had called Rebecca the night before to notify her that her mother's killer had been found. She'd hurried down to the police station once she got the news, and we'd had a chance to talk in a hallway.

"Thank you for everything," she'd said, pulling me into a hug. "You've done so much to help me. How can I ever repay you?"

"I was just doing what was right. You should focus on yourself right now and getting out of your marriage. How are things going with that?"

"Pretty well, actually. I was connected with a lawyer who's been really helpful, and David has said he'll do whatever I ask of him. The county is likely to still press charges against him for assaulting that officer, so at least I don't have to worry about him trying to weasel his way back into my life while I get a divorce."

"I'm glad to hear it. Any luck finding the money your mother hid?"

"Not yet, but I'm going to keep looking. Honestly, I want to spend this time with my mother's belongings, remembering the woman she was. The money would be nice, but I want to savor her memory more."

"I hope it turns up for you, and that you get the closure you need. Try to take care of yourself, too, okay?"

Back at the bistro, Estelle popped her head into the room and hurried over once she spotted us.

"Where have you been?" I asked, scooting over to make room for her at the table.

"At the police station," she said, out of breath from her rush back here.

"Really? Why did you go back?" I asked. Miles reached over and squeezed his wife's hand, and Eddy drifted away to clear plates from another table.

"I wanted to talk to them about a volunteer opportunity. I've been thinking a lot about Kathleen and our friendship since last night. I'm still sad she's gone, of course, but now that we've found the killer, I know she wouldn't want me sitting around, grieving her death. She'd want me to continue living my life and being happy. After all this, I'm feeling reinvigorated and ready to take on the whole world."

"Well, I'm glad to hear that," I said. "What led you to the police station? Did they have more questions for you?"

She shook her head. "Like I said, I'm interested in volunteering. We've been investigating all these murders on our own for so long, and after last night, I'm ready to get a little closer to the action!"

"I thought you said it was going to be a paperwork gig?" Miles asked, his gaze concerned.

"It is," Estelle said slowly. "I'm going to help them catalog some of their cold cases. But this way, I can learn more about all the crimes happening in town sooner, and maybe I can help solve them faster!"

Oh, jeez. I bet the police had no idea what they were

getting into when they agreed to let Estelle volunteer with them. Hopefully this new job would keep her from trying to drag me into more murder investigations. I was tired of having guns waved in my face and my life threatened. Unless, of course, Estelle managed to find a cold case to get me involved in...

I pushed away thoughts about getting caught up in more murder investigations. Right now, I was celebrating our safety with my friends. All of that other messy stuff could wait until later. I was simply glad that Estelle was finally able to move on and grieve Kathleen like she deserved. She'd finally found a way to process everything that had happened.

"You look very lovely today," Estelle said with a quirky smile, gesturing to my dress. "Any special plans?"

I rolled my eyes with a laugh and smoothed out the purple dress. "My mom's idea. She came to my apartment early this morning and suggested I wear it to, and I quote, 'celebrate catching a killer.' I told her it was a pretty kooky idea, but she thought it might help me get into the holiday spirit."

"Well, I think it's gorgeous," Estelle said, looping her arm through Miles's and smirking at him.

I narrowed my eyes, wondering what she wasn't saying, when my mom entered the bistro and walked over to our table, grabbing another seat. She waved to Eddy to bring her a coffee, then smiled up at the rest of the table. "Glad to see everyone is still alive this morning," she said with a chuckle. "I can't say I expected my trip to take a turn like it has, but I'm glad to be here spending the holidays with you all."

I smiled and squeezed her hand, nodding my agreement. I was happy to have my mom around for the holiday season this year. We'd been through a lot during the past week, and I hoped the rest of her trip wouldn't be as exciting. I was glad we'd had a chance to talk about Sylvia's letter, and I felt even closer to her after knowing about what had happened between the two sisters. I hoped nothing like that happened with Chrissy and me.

"And you're wearing the dress!" she added with a squeal, clapping her hands together. "It looks so good on you."

"Yes, I was just telling her how pretty she looks," Estelle said, winking at my mom.

I pursed my lips. Okay, now Estelle was *winking* at people? What was going on with everyone and this dress?

"Nadia!" Penny's voice cut through the din of the bistro, and our attention swiveled to the main door, thoughts of my fancy dress flying out of my head. Nadia entered the bistro and waved hello, letting out an *oomph!* of surprise when Penny launched herself into the other woman's arms for a hug.

I laughed and strode over to the two women, pulling Nadia into a hug once Penny was finished. "I didn't think we were going to see you again until after New Year's," I said, patting her back.

"And miss Christmas at the Hemlock? Never." She smiled, her gaze turning serious. "Listen, Simone, do you mind if we talk privately? It'll just take a second."

"Sure," I replied as Penny drifted away to clear the plates on another table. "Do you want to go to my office?"

"No, here's fine." She pulled us to a corner of the bistro and lowered her voice. "I really appreciate you letting me take this time off to be with Christos. I know this is our busiest season, and I'm sure it wasn't easy managing all the guests with one less staff member."

"Don't worry at all, we managed." I decided not to

mention the murder investigation and chaos at the inn from the last few days. She was still glowing from her trip, and I didn't want to spoil it for her.

She let out a sigh, visibly relieved at my words. "That's good to hear. I love working at the Hemlock, and I can see myself being here for a really long time. But...I also want to spend more time with Christos. Not another two-month cruise," she added quickly, seeing the concern flash across my face. "But we want to try to make things less long-distance between us and see each other more often, so I might plan more weekends away. I know Tracy is planning a vacation next year with Isabella, so I hate even asking, but I just really love Christos..." Her voice trailed off, her gaze nervous as she waited for my response.

Laughing, I pulled her into another hug. "Of course you should spend time with your boyfriend! I want you to have a good life with him. I know I can run this place, and I want the people around me to be happy."

Nadia squeezed me back. "Oh, that's so great to hear. Thank you so much."

She stepped away to give Estelle and Miles a hug, and I smiled as I watched the reunion. It was good to have her back, but I also knew she needed to have a life outside of the inn, too. So did I, in fact. I finally felt like I'd gotten to a place where I was ready to move onto the next stage of my relationship with Nick. Now if only he were around to talk about it.

I'd tried calling him late last night, after everything had finished at the crime scene and the police station, but he hadn't answered—probably sleeping. I'd try to find him today to talk about moving in together, and maybe more...

"Simone, do you mind helping me with something?" Tracy appeared at the bistro door and waved me over.

"Of course." I waved goodbye to my table of friends and followed her out into the lobby.

"I pulled this box down from one of the closets," she explained, leading me over to a cardboard box sitting by the Christmas tree in the lobby. "More decorations that I missed before. Mind helping me add the last ones to the tree?"

"No problem," I said, pulling out a red glass ball and hanging it from the tree. "Although, I gotta say...don't you think there are enough decorations on this tree? I mean, I'm kinda worried about it toppling over from the weight of them all!"

Tracy laughed, hanging up a reindeer cutout. "You might be right, but I can't help it. I love this holiday so much, and decorating the tree has always been my favorite tradition. To me, there's no such thing as too many decorations."

"Maybe you're right." I chuckled, adding a silver glass ball to the tree. "Hey, listen, I wanted to talk about your trip. I know I said I was fine with it, and I am, I promise, but I'm also nervous about you leaving the inn for so long. I don't want to hold things back anymore, so I wanted to tell you that I am a bit scared."

Tracy set down the ornament she'd been fiddling with and pulled me into a hug. "I appreciate you saying something. Thank you for being honest with me. But I know you'll do a great job here on your own. You are an amazing business owner, and you've got a great staff working with you. You'll be okay, I promise."

"Thanks. I think you're right, but I wanted to say it. I'm so excited for you and Isabella."

"Me too! Besides, this trip won't be forever. I need this time away from the inn and from remembering Sylvia everywhere I look. I'm hoping I'll come back reinvigorated and ready to take this place to the next level. Besides, if you need anything, I'm just a phone call away."

"You're right. I hope this trip is everything you wish it to be. And there, that's the last one." I added the last decoration to the tree and took a step back to survey our work. "Not bad at all."

"Oh, also, I talked to your mom about Sylvia," Tracy added, lowering her voice. "I know I'd been avoiding saying anything, so I finally felt like I had to talk to her about our past relationship. She was so supportive and understanding. I'm glad I said something."

"That's great to hear! See, I told you it wouldn't be so scary. And now you can go on this trip knowing that you got all these things off your chest."

"You're right," Tracy said with a smile. Her gaze shifted to something over my shoulder, and her smile widened. "Looks like there's someone here to talk to you," she said, pointing over my shoulder.

I turned around as Nick came through the doors of the lobby, looking around nervously. I hurried over to him and pulled him into a hug.

"It's so good to see you," I said, nestling my face in his neck. I was glad he'd gotten my messages and come by the Hemlock.

"How are you doing?" he asked, holding me out at arms' length and inspecting for any injuries.

I laughed. "Much better, now that you're here. I promise I'm not hurt. Want to get some breakfast and hear all about my night?"

"In a minute. There's, um, something I wanted to talk about. Let's go into the bistro." He led me into the other room, which was now empty of guests. Where had everyone gone?

Instead of people, all the tables had been cleared and pushed back against the walls. Twinkle lights were strung up around the ceiling—those looked like the twinkle lights that Tracy had leant Nick earlier in the week.

I turned back to my boyfriend, a question on my face, and noticed his suit and tie. A bow tie, actually. Blue, just like the one that he'd received from Hank at his farm, and the same as what Hank had worn during the pie contest in the spring. I knew it looked familiar.

"What's going on?" I asked slowly, trying to put together the pieces of Nick in a bowtie, twinkle lights strung up around the bistro, and everyone cleared out. Was he about to…?

He held my hands, his palms sweaty. "Um, I wanted to apologize for being so absent this week, especially with your mom being here. I've been talking to a lot of people, about us and our relationship. I, uh, I talked to your parents. I wanted your mom to be here for this. She and my dad really hit it off, too." He smiled sheepishly, and my grip tightened around his fingers. Was that how my mom had known Kenji's name before I told her? She'd talked to Nick?

"What's going on?" I repeated, my heartbeat thudding in my chest.

"I'm glad you're safe. I love you so much, and I can't stop thinking about you. I'm proud of everything you've done at this inn, and I love how willing you are to help the people around you to find justice for them, even if it scares me when you risk your life like that." He reached into his pocket and pulled something out, keeping his hand down by his side. "The reason I've been absent this week is because I've been shopping around, trying to find the right option. I wanted to get something perfect for you, because you deserve the best."

He dropped down to one knee, and I gasped, my heart skipping a beat. Over his head, I saw Estelle, my mom gripping a camera, ready to take a photo, Kenji, Tracy, and all my other friends from Pine Brook gathered in the entryway to the bistro behind us. My eyes filled with tears as I settled them back on Nick.

"I wanted to do this somewhere special for us both," Nick went on, his smile slowly widening. "This is where we first met, you remember that?"

I nodded slowly, too stunned to speak. Of course I remembered meeting Nick for the first time, how could I forget? I never could've imagined after that first meeting, when our eyes had locked and I'd felt a spark course through me, that I'd be standing here with him again all this time later, dolled up in a fancy dress, my friends and family watching close by, while he spoke words that sent a shiver down my spine.

"I want to spend the rest of my life with you, and I hope you'll give me that honor. Simone, will you marry me?"

A million emotions ran through me at those words, but without any hesitation, the most important word slipped from my mouth:

"Yes!"

EPILOGUE

Six months later, I sat in one of the larger suites in the inn, fiddling with my white dress while Chrissy added the finishing touches to my makeup. She took a step back and cocked her head to the side, smiling as she studied my face.

"I think we're done." She held up a mirror for me. "You look perfect."

"Thank you," I said, admiring the amazing job she'd done in the mirror. "Let's hope this lasts through the night!"

"Don't worry, it'll be perfect," she said with a laugh. "Hannah, come tell your Aunt Simone she looks gorgeous."

My young niece, Hannah, hurried over from where she'd been playing with some toys, her basket of flower petals clutched in one hand. "You look beautiful," she said, gazing up at me with a smile. I bent and kissed her forehead, rubbing her back.

"Thank you. Your mom did a great job."

"I can't believe it's finally here," Chrissy said, coming to sit next to me on the bench. "Are you ready?"

Christmas and Killers

I smoothed out my dress and took a couple deep breaths. "I think I am. I can't believe I'm finally marrying my best friend."

Chrissy laughed and stood, starting to pack up her makeup kit. "Don't let Estelle hear you call him your best friend. She's already claimed that title."

I laughed and studied my makeup in the mirror, being careful not to smudge anything. The last six months had passed by in a blur of wedding planning and running the inn. Tracy had had a wonderful time on her trip, returning to Pine Brook the week before, just in time for the wedding. We'd managed to go the entire time without any murders in town, and I had a strong feeling that today was going to go perfectly.

The inn had flourished in the last few months. Even with Tracy gone and me planning a wedding, we were busier than we'd ever been, all of our rooms booked out every week, more and more people showing up to the bistro, and the spa offering even more services every month. I'd had a lot of help planning the wedding, fortunately, so I'd been able to focus a lot of my attention on making the inn as successful as possible. Hank had even made us a wedding cake, after his catering business on the side had officially launched after the holidays. Now he was making birthday pies, wedding cakes, and yummy scones, for anyone who wanted to spice up their celebrations.

Tracy had arrived back from her trip with Isabella as rejuvenated as she'd hoped she'd be, and I'd sensed she was ready for the next step in her relationship with Isabella. When Tracy had squealed over a picture of kid's shoes in a magazine in the lobby, I'd had a feeling I knew where things were going next for them. They were both a bit too old for pregnancy—and neither seemed all that eager to be pregnant, anyway—but I had a feeling Tracy had started browsing adoption websites in her spare time.

When I'd arrived at the Hemlock that morning, giddy about my upcoming nuptials, I'd found Eddy and Penny in the lobby arranging flowers to display for the ceremony. Eddy's boyfriend was helping them out, and I'd been thrilled to see more of him the past few weeks as planning for the wedding sped up.

Because business was booming, Penny had been helping out more and more at the spa, and she'd started researching massage schools to get her license. While we'd miss her in the bistro, she'd always had such a calming presence and would do a great job of helping people relax and ease tension from their bodies.

I'd also passed by Nadia in the courtyard, putting together party favor bags with Christos by her side. The two waved to me as I passed. She'd been taking off more time to spend with Christos, who'd finally moved to Pine Brook to be closer to her. But rather than miss her presence when she was gone, she'd instead stepped up even more at the inn and taken on more responsibly, making things easier for me as the owner.

If I ever decided to expand the inn or open up a new location somewhere else, Nadia would do an excellent job with getting us set up someplace new. She'd really grown so much in the time I'd been working with her, and I was so proud to see it.

My mom poked her head into the room where I was getting ready. "Almost done?" she asked, her gaze landing on me. "Oh, you look beautiful, my dear." She came over and gave me a hug, squeezing tight.

"I think we're about ready," Chrissy said, packing up her

bag. "I'll go let Estelle know she should start getting everyone seated."

It had been an easy decision to pick Estelle as our officiant, and she'd eagerly snatched up the job. I couldn't wait to see what she had planned for us.

She and Miles were as in love as they'd ever been, and thrilled to help plan my wedding. Estelle had turned into an excellent volunteer at the police station, and she and Miriam had even managed to update and modernize parts of the station that were still in the past. Even Chief Tate had to admit that they'd improved things and made the station more efficient and productive. Miles, of course, still spent most of his time with Lola and playing chess, and he was happy that his wife was so happy.

Once we were alone, my mom turned to me. "Are you ready? This is a big step. I know I was nervous on my wedding day."

"Honestly, I'm not that nervous. I mean, these heels are pretty tall, so we'll see if I can make it down the aisle, but I feel ready to do this."

"Excellent. Then let's get out there, okay?" She stood and held out her arm, which I took, then she led me out of the suite and towards the back of the inn.

We'd transformed the outdoor area near the spa into a gorgeous garden for the wedding, and I knew it was going to work perfectly for us to hold future weddings at the inn, too.

My dad met us as we passed through the lobby, and he came to grip my arm from the other side. "You look beautiful," he whispered. "I'm so proud of all you've accomplished."

"Thank you," I murmured back, my eyes already filled with tears.

"Nick is a lucky man. Don't let him forget it," he added

with a wink, then the three of us walked outside and down the aisle.

We'd invited less than a hundred people, but it felt like thousands were waiting for us at the aisle, everyone standing as they watched us walk down. My breath caught in my throat as I saw all the people, feeling overwhelmed by so many faces looking up at me.

But then, I spotted Eddy in the crowd, and Tracy, and Nadia. I smiled at all the faces, all these people who loved me and wanted to see me get married today. I could handle anything.

I'd invited Detective Patel to the wedding—how could I not?—but she'd unfortunately not been able to attend. While I was sad she couldn't be here with us, I knew she was where she needed to be right now, in Seattle training new police officers on how to be good cops.

And then, there he was—Nick stood at the end of the aisle, next to Estelle, looking ravishing in a tuxedo. He fiddled with his lapel, then stilled as he saw me walk down the aisle. Kenji was seated next to Miles in the front row, and my future father-in-law squeezed my hand as I passed by.

I hugged my mom and dad once we made it down the aisle, then went to stand next to Nick, holding his hands in mine. We both turned our attention to Estelle, who began to speak.

I'd come to Pine Brook unsure about what I was doing with my life or the kind of person I wanted to be. And I'd stayed because of all the murder I was getting caught up in.

But really, I stayed because of the people around me. All the wonderful friends and family I'd made since coming to Washington were what kept me here, and I was thrilled to be committing to Nick in this way. I didn't know what the future would hold for us, but I was so happy to be spending this day with him and all of our friends.

This was truly the happiest day of my life.

THANKS FOR READING!

I hope you've enjoyed spending time with Simone and the Hemlock Inn! It would mean the world to me if you could recommend this series to another friend.

ACKNOWLEDGMENTS

Many thanks to my editor, Carmen, for always knowing exactly what these books need to make them shine on the page, and thanks to my friends and family for all their support over the past few years.

Immense gratitude do all my readers: I've so enjoyed writing these books for you, and I'm so grateful to all of you who have stuck around. Writing a book can be such a solitary endeavor, but knowing that I have readers who are eager for the next book keeps me motivated and loving what I do.

As of June 2022, I'm working on a new mystery series, which I hope to share with you in the coming months. Follow me on social media (find me on Facebook or Instagram), or join my newsletter at www.josephinesmithauthor.com to stay up-to-date on my books!

ABOUT THE AUTHOR

Josephine Smith is an author of cozy mysteries. A Washington state native, Josephine now makes her home in Northern California with her husband and dog and cat. She loves all things sweet, foods and people included, and can be found with her nose buried in a book. Visit her website at www.josephinesmithauthor.com, or connect on social media at Josephine Smith, Author (Facebook and Instagram).

Come say hello!

ALSO BY JOSEPHINE SMITH

The Hemlock Inn Mysteries series

Auctions and Alibis

College and Criminals

Medicine and Murder

Bakers and Bloodshed

Galleries and Gunmen

Christmas and Killers

Made in United States
Troutdale, OR
02/25/2024

17964283R00128